THREE FORGOTTEN TALES

Jon Ferguson

Huge Jam Publishing, 2022
England

VOL. 1

JESUS & MARY

If a tiny omniscient insect crawled into your ear one cozy star-filled night and whispered, "Friend of this world, I must tell you that there are no historical facts," would this change anything about your life? If the insect then decided to stay a while and explain what it meant, would you listen? Would you care to hear what it meant? Would you let the insect metamorphose your whole view of the very idea of "history"? Would you let the insect scratch your eardrum with its tiny hands and feet until you understood what it meant? Most people would never understand, but for those who would, here is a story of Jesus and Mary Magdalene.

PREFACE

Everything ever written about Mary Magdalene is false. Everything ever written about Jesus is false. Everything ever written about history is false for history is not a ball of string that unwinds in a straight line for people to touch, see, and understand. Every moment is infinitely complex. Everything is attached to everything else. How many moments has history had? How much Being is in every moment? There is not enough time and not enough words to describe any single moment of history. When anybody tries to explain anything they are trying to squeeze the universe into their own glass jar. Anyone who claims to be able to do this is a charlatan, gentle or otherwise.

The life of the man they call Jesus is a very good

example. What does anyone really know about Jesus? He was said to be the son of God. What does anyone know about God? He was said to be born of a virgin mother. No one knows if this is true. No one knows anything about his mother's sex life. Anyone could say his mother was a virgin. I had a cousin who got pregnant and her devout Christian parents said she never had sex, but that an errant sperm had crept inside her vagina. Was this "true"?

You and I are alive today. Does anybody really know anything about us? Does anyone understand the inter-workings of the millions of atoms and cells that we are "made of"? Of course not. And our hearts and minds? Even people who live with us don't have a clue as to what transpires in the depths of our souls. The world is a gargantuan secret. Jesus lived two thousand years ago. Think of how his life has been warped by millions of interpretations that have nothing to do with the truth. Nobody will ever know the truth. People just use other people to fit their version of the truth. People use "history" to fit their version of what life is all about. But there is no knowable history, and life can never fit into that glass jar.

My story of the love affair between Mary

Magdalene and Jesus is what I imagine happened. Nobody has to agree with me. I don't want any followers. I don't want to start a new religion or destroy an old one. More lies have probably been told about Jesus than any other person who has ever walked the earth. There are hundreds of versions of his life. Most people will buy into the version that confirms what they happen to believe about life and truth. I don't believe in Christianity, but sometimes I like to believe in Jesus. Like Nietzsche said, "There was only one Christian and he died on the cross."

Le voici…

1

There are no books except a few copies of the Old Testament written on parchment. There are no newspapers, televisions, radios, magazines, iPads, podcasts or phones. Computers, cameras, cars, trains, airplanes, bicycles, and electric light bulbs will be invented a couple of thousand years later. There are no vaccinations against diseases and medicine men have absolutely no idea about what goes on under the skin. No one has ever heard of a gun or a bomb. All wars are fought face to face. People don't know that a baby is made when a sperm penetrates an egg. Most men die before the age of forty, women before thirty. The world is flat and not much bigger than Liechtenstein. Few people have been more than a few miles from where they were born. Nobody has heard of an atom or a cell. Leibnitz won't be born for seventeen centuries. The word gravity means nothing. There are no sharp needles with which to sew clothes. One pair of shoes is a lot. You bathe in a river or a lake or the sea. Only the sun heats the water. There is no toilet paper. For that matter, there are no toilets. No one has ever heard of a Pope, a Catholic, a Crusade, a Muslim, a Mormon, a Christian, an Evolution or a Big Bang. Olives are a food staple. People get born in mangers. No one calls the area around Jerusalem "holy".

There is a lot going on elsewhere on the planet Earth, but the people in and around Jerusalem don't know about it. The people in the other parts of the earth don't know about Jerusalem.

11

That's just the way it was back then. A few thousand years down the road, today will look the same.

III

Isn't it interesting how the farther away myths and traditions get, the more people believe them. Shortly after Jesus died, nobody believed he was God's son or a miracle worker. Nobody believed he died to save the world from sin. Most people didn't have a clue about what sin was. They were just trying to survive. Sure there was the Jewish tradition and the Old Testament. But the Romans had most of the power. They wielded the big sticks. As they slowly self-destructed and whittled themselves away, the whole Christian thing started to take root. But it had no roots when Jesus died.

IV

Forget the wise men and the virgin. Jesus was born like every other kid, on a straw bed. His mother was nervous but loving. His father had a pleasant disposition, a bad leg, and tendency toward laziness. Jesus's childhood was normal: no broken arms or legs, lots of bread and olives, stories about Adam and Eve and the Ten Commandments. He was special because he had an inquisitive mind. He tended to doubt much of what he heard. He asked lots of questions. When they said Moses made the Red Sea open up, he thought it probably never happened. When they said God made the world in six days, then rested, he thought they had no proof. If God were almighty why would He even need to rest? Why six days? Why didn't He have slaves do the work like the Romans did? And he knew the Romans had other stories and other gods to explain where everybody came from. When he reached age sixteen, he had no idea about what was true and false. He just looked at the world and observed the life that was in front of him: blue sky, sun, hills, paths, people, moon, goats, cats, dogs, stars, insects, trees, flowers, grass, rain, clouds, suffering, pain, laughter, birth, death, happiness, sadness. When he saw a creature die, it didn't look like it was going anywhere.

What was the sky? What was that vast sheet of blue, grey, and black above him? What was in it? At night, what glittered? He took walks. He wondered why, and how, and what. He had no answers. Sometimes the moon was bigger than other times. Were there two moons? Three? Four? Sometimes it was a half-circle. Sometimes just a slice. He got dizzy. People told him it wasn't worth getting dizzy about. God created it. But Jesus doubted God, any and all gods. The Romans had lots of them. How big was it all? Did it end?

When he was seventeen he started watching himself think. Did thinking happen in the eye, the head, the ears, the heart, the groin? Maybe it came from every part of the body. Maybe God put thoughts in people's heads. Maybe the thinking invented God. Did animals think? In any case a lot of thoughts came out of people's mouths. He listened to what people said. Most of what they said had to do with themselves. That made some kind of sense.

Jesus was friends with everybody — Pharisees, Romans, slaves, old, young, men, women, children, animals. He wandered a lot and watched the world. Everybody had his or her story to tell. He was a good listener. His world was small. Stories overlapped and intertwined. The same words and people came up over and over again.

Jesus's mother and father were both dead before he was eleven. His mother died first, at the age of twenty-nine, after giving birth to a girl, a half-sister. His father was much older than his mother. He had had two other children with another woman before fathering Jesus. He died an old man at age fifty-seven.

Back then kids weren't babied like they are today. You had to fend for yourself early. Which reminds me of something I read in a history book the other day. Did you know that in the twelfth century there was something called "The Children's Crusade"? 30,000 children between the ages of six and twelve were walking together across what is now France to get to Jerusalem. When they arrived in Marseille they were put in boats. Two of the boats sank and everyone on them died. The other boats went to Northern Africa where the children were all sold off as slaves.

V

Mary is seventeen, twelve years younger than Jesus. Her eyes are small turquoise oceans that see much of the same world Jesus sees. (Jesus didn't see the uncle or the Roman soldier who came to rape her.) Males are moved when she walks by. Her clothes are like sacks; men try to see through them. She has been on her own since she was seven, sleeping and eating wherever she can. At first she was like a wild animal, only seeing out and seeking to survive. Now she has started to reflect and she loves Jesus. She wonders what moves heads and hearts, particularly her own. She eventually wonders what moves everything — moon, sun, fish, snake, bird, finger, foot, cloud, Roman, uncle, donkey, tree…

Over the years they have crossed paths many

times, but neither she nor Jesus has ever dared or wanted to stop. But on this day when they see each other their eyes stick. Does it matter why? He knows her name is Mary like his mother's. His head is slightly tilted as he walks towards her to speak. "Mary, I have finished my work for the day. Would you like to walk with me?"

They leave the village and climb a hill to a place where they can look out over the land. It is early evening and the sun is behind them. When she speaks, he is reminded of trees in the wind…

I know a little about you. Your father was Joseph.
Yes. He is dead.
You seem to have lots of friends. Every time I see you, you have people around you.
I am nice to people. I see no reason to treat people badly.
Even the Romans?
The Romans didn't ask to be Romans. They're only doing their job.
I wish they would do it elsewhere.
Someone will always have power. What's more important is the power you have over yourself.
When they rape you your power gets lost.

They shouldn't rape you, but "shouldn't" is a word that doesn't have much meaning.

They are pigs.

Men are animals.

Worse.

Not always.

Of course.

Have they raped you?

Once. A soldier followed me to where I was sleeping. I woke up in the middle of the night and he was lying next to me. I smelled him before I saw him. He told me not to make a noise and everything would be all right. I hate the Romans. I'm lucky it's only happened once with them.

Has it happened with anyone else?

My uncle. He isn't really my uncle. He is my half-brother. I call him my uncle because he's fifteen years older than me. He's also your brother.

What do you mean?

Your half-brother. He's your father's son.

How do you know?

My mother told me that Joseph fathered David then left her. She was young. Younger than I am now.

How old are you?

Seventeen.

I know this David. My father never told me he was my brother.

In the end we're all brothers and sisters.

And David, did he rape you?

He forced himself on me. I was fifteen, the same age as my mother was when she had Joseph's baby.

But there was no baby?

No.

And the Roman soldier? There was no baby?

No.

So, you are not a prostitute? I'd been told that sometimes you sell your body.

All women are prostitutes. That is, all women who make love when they don't want to are prostitutes. If they don't do it for money they do it for a home, security, family, food… It's the same thing.

And you?

I've given my body for coins when I was hungry.

I can't imagine making love to a woman who didn't want to make love with me.

You must be lucky then and have women who want you. She looked away from him when she said this and stared out into the desert.

Not recently… he mused. *And I really don't understand people who do things against other people's wills.*

Wills often collide. Most men don't think before they act.

Fools know not what they do.

Why do you think God lets bad things happen?

What is bad for one is good for another.

Why would God let men kill each other?

If He existed, I don't think He would.

You don't think He exists?

I have no idea. But if He does exist and He lets people rape you, He is a strange God.

The Jewish God is very strange, destroying lots of things, getting mad and throwing His thunderbolts.

That's why I only pretend I'm a Jew. I really don't believe in any of it.

You don't believe in Heaven and Hell?

I can't believe God would punish people. The idea of Hell is barbaric. The Jews try to frighten people to get them to follow their rules. Why would God want to frighten people? I can only imagine a god trying to help people. Like a mother or a good father.

Maybe God isn't nice. The Romans have many gods and some of them are cruel.

Yes, I know.

Jesus, do you think there's the one single god... or

many gods?

How could anyone know?

But people pretend to know. Why?

Because they can't help themselves. Their minds are small. Are you thirsty? There's a stream not far from here.

Yes, actually I am.

Let's go then.

As they rose he took her hand.

VI

Mary and Jesus saw each other the next day. It was the Sabbath. Friday? Saturday? Sunday? What difference does it make? The universe has no idea what day it is. Nobody knows when the earth's spinning started. But we sure like to think we do.

VII

If you wish to have any chance of understanding what this book is trying to say, you must remove all preconceived ideas about Jesus based on your own twentieth or twenty-first century life. Most people in the Occident concoct their idea of Jesus from what goes on (or went on) in their church and on two major holidays, Christmas and Easter. Let's forget Easter for now and think about the way we imagine Jesus based on our celebration of his birth every year on the twenty-fifth of December:

First we see the Virgin Mary, her nice quiet husband Joseph, and the little baby Jesus in Mary's arms all warm and cosy in an open barn, with a hay-filled manger. Everybody is happy and healthy. Jesus never cries and Mary looks like she just dressed after a warm bath. There is no doctor in sight, but there are three wise men (why are they wise? – what wise things have they ever said? – of course we have no idea about any of that) who have brought wonderful gifts. Then we see the heavenly star above the blessed stable shining divine light on the whole scene. This is how we perceive the birth of Jesus. Then we add the Christmas tree in the living room with all the lights, candles, glittering balls and tinsel. Now throw in the presents under the tree, many bought and wrapped with much thought and love. On top of that add the best meal of the year that mother has spent all day preparing. And finally turn on the stereo and hear some of the most beautiful peaceful songs ever written sung by the amazing voices of Bing Crosby, Mahalia Jackson, Johnny Mathis, Barbara Hendricks, Placido Domingo, or the Mormon Tabernacle Choir… This is CHRISTmas — the glorious concept shines in your head for the rest of your life!

You will never be able to dissociate the Christmas holiday from your idea of Jesus. But this idea has absolutely nothing to do with the birth and life of Jesus. It is total myth. Nobody is suggesting that myths are bad. They might be the most necessary things in human society. But they have nothing to do with truth and what actually happened in the world.

Jesus was probably born with great pain to the mother. There was no special star above the barn. There were no wise men coming on camels in the moonlight. (Maybe Jesus was born at ten o'clock in the morning.) Joseph might have been nowhere in sight.

No one will ever know the circumstances of Jesus's birth. But it most surely has nothing to do with the atmosphere of Christmas as we celebrate it today.

Now think of the Jesus that we hear about in our Christian churches. Think of the painted pictures on the walls. Jesus always has that nice beard and flowing clean long hair. Probably every man in Jesus's time had a beard and nobody had clean hair. Then the stories of Jesus, the miracles, the walking on water, feeding five thousand people with a few loaves of bread, healing lepers and other people stuck with pathetic lives. None of this is likely any truer than the myths about Jesus's birth. We must wipe all this from our heads and try to clean the slate.

Who was Jesus? What was the world like two thousand years ago? We'll never know, but we're trying to imagine as best we can. Remember, Jesus's world was small, like Rhode Island, and flat. No one had a clue what was going on over the rest of the planet. Just like us today… we have no idea what is going on in the rest of the universe. Jesus's universe was Nazareth, Jerusalem, Galilee, Bethlehem, the sky directly overhead, and nothing else. Nobody had a clue where any of it came from. Nobody in Jesus's world had been to Africa, America, China, even Turkey, Greece, or Europe. They hadn't even been to Syria, Egypt, or Iraq. Our universe is Earth, Mars, Jupiter, the Milky Way, 13,000,000,000 years of evolution, black holes, and a few more galaxies. Nobody knows what's really out there, way out there! Or how long it's been there. 2,000 years from now – the same amount of calendar time we are from Jesus – people will have a totally different view of life and the universe.

It's all about perspective. We have ours. Jesus had his. Back to his…

VIII

Jesus and Mary met again in the olive grove on the hill overlooking Nazareth. Though it was the Sabbath neither went into the synagogue before or after their rendezvous. Jesus didn't believe he needed a rabbi to tell him what was good or bad, right or wrong, true or false. As far as he was concerned the rabbis didn't know any more than he did about anything. They thought their thoughts, he thought his. Also, he didn't like crowds of people. He never wanted others to speak or act for him, especially not a mob. He had seen many times how mobs became violent and thoughtless. Remember, Jesus was a doubter and a thinker. He was also twenty-nine years old. He'd had time to wonder, wander, marvel, and think about his world.

As they sat in the sunburnt grass under the olive tree, Jesus noticed how beautiful Mary Magdalene was. She was seventeen. Though she had been raped twice (actually many more times if you consider all the times she let men have her in order to get something to eat), her face showed no signs or scars of misery or suffering. Only every now and then Jesus would notice a vertical crease appear above her nose which might reveal some small hint of worry or dismay. Her skin was like the petal of a flower, he thought. When she talked, she would often wet her lips between sentences. All he wanted to do was kiss her, but he didn't because he didn't want to be like other men who had precipitously thrown themselves on her because of her beauty. He could wait forever because he loved her.

Where's your mother?

I don't know. She went away with a man when I was too young to remember. I don't know if the man forced her to go or not. She left me with her sister, who died when I was nine or ten. I'm not sure exactly. I was left to fend for myself. For years I was like a stray dog just trying to find food and a place to sleep. I often slept next to that rock over there (she points with a long, lovely finger on her left hand.)

Jesus rejoined. *I was fortunate. When my mother died, I still had my father and eventually he gave me work. He was rather lazy, so he was happy when I was old enough to do things for him.*

What was his work?

He made tables and chairs and cupboards. I must have started working when I was eleven. I still work sometimes as I need money to eat. I sleep in the same house I've always slept in. It's one room, but the roof over it is strong and rain never gets in. You must see it one day.

I would like to. Do you have children? Do you live alone?

I have no children that I know of. There are travelers who sometimes stay with me, but not for long. And you, Mary… Do you have children?

I was with child once, I think. I was sick in the morning for a few weeks. Then something happened. I bled a lot and whatever was inside me was gone.

You said you were "like a stray dog."

Yes, I was.

One thing that fascinates me is the difference – or lack of difference – between men and animals. What qualities do men have that animals don't have? And what qualities do animals have that men don't have? How are we alike? How are we different?

It depends on which man and which animal. I have known men who act like animals and I've seen animals that appear to act like men. Both men and animals can be gentle. Both men and animals can be cruel and violent.

I am fascinated by birds. No man can fly. No man can pass from tree to tree without putting his feet back on the ground.

Do you think God created animals for man?

Who's even to say God created animals? Maybe animals created God. Maybe neither was created? I have no idea.

All the rabbis say God created man, then animals, then plants and trees.

What do the rabbis know?

I don't know.

And what might this god they talk about be? They talk about God as if he were their best friend. As if they know what He is like and how He acts. Maybe God is nothing like they describe. Maybe there is no God. They have never seen this God. Maybe their God has a god over Him. Maybe birds are the real gods. Mary, for me it is all a big mystery, bigger than any mind can imagine. Mary takes Jesus's hand and holds it to her breast.

I've never heard anyone talk that way before, Jesus.

And I have never had anyone listen the way you listen, Mary. Few people want to hear me.

I will hear you.

And I will hear you, Jesus said.

IX

Both Mary and Jesus took the long way home after they separated. Jesus had brought a loaf of bread and some olives and they had drunk wine. Both had finished eating for the day. There was about an hour of sunlight left. Before going to sleep each wanted to be alone with the thought of the other. When a body fills with love the rest of the human world can be a great cacophony.

Mary lived with a woman who had four children – all girls between the ages of six and twelve – and a dying old man. The woman said the man was her father. She said that years ago her husband had been beaten by the Romans for refusing to give them the family donkey. The soldiers took the husband away, but "miraculously" left the donkey. For the past six months Mary had been sleeping in the departed husband's bed. Every morning, except the Sabbath, she would feed and wash the old man while the woman and her daughters went to the market to sell the vegetables that grow behind the house. The donkey transported the goods.

As she walked on the path on the edge of the town, Mary was so engrossed in her thoughts about the man she had spent the afternoon with that she didn't look behind her to see if she was being followed. She had three thoughts spinning through her mind. First, *"Is it possible that there is no god who created and rules over the earth?"* Second, *"If there is no god in heaven, must I find a god on earth?"* Third, *"Jesus is not like other men. He could be my god on earth and I could be his goddess… for as long as we live."*

Fortunately, no one was following her. She got home just as darkness enveloped Nazareth. The woman was concerned about her. The girls were already asleep in their corner of the hut.

Mary, I was worried about you.

I'm completely fine. In fact, I had a wonderful afternoon.

Have you eaten enough?

Yes, thank you. But I'd like some water. I have walked a long way.

Of course. There is enough for tonight and the morning.

I was with the man named Jesus. Do you know him?

Yes, I do know who he is. I have seen him in the market. He is kind, but very strange. Sometimes he buys vegetables and then immediately gives them away to the poor.

We spent the afternoon talking. He says things I've never heard another man say. He doesn't believe in the Jewish God. He doesn't believe there is a Heaven or a Hell. He thinks that when you die that is the end. He says life is a mystery, but it is very possible that this life is all we have.

How can a man not believe in God or Heaven or Hell? He is a Jew, isn't he?

He says there is no reason to believe the rabbis.

Then who should we believe? The Romans…?

No, not the Romans. But he doesn't hate them. He says they're only doing their job and that they did not ask to be born Roman. What they do is not their fault. He says if Jews had been born Romans, they'd be doing the same things.

The Romans are stupid.

Jesus thinks everybody is stupid. Not stupid in a bad way. But stupid like animals.

Did he try to take advantage of your body?

No, not for a second. It was I who pulled his hand to my breast. I was the first to touch his flesh.

I don't believe you Mary.

It's true. We were alone in the olive orchard. We talked. We listened to each other. I've never had such a conversation. I've never felt such things in the presence of a man.

He cannot be a good man if he doesn't believe in God.

But so many bad men believe in God. The Romans believe in God.

They believe in gods… the wrong gods. They don't believe in Jehovah.

Why are the Roman gods wrong and the Jewish god right? That's the kind of question Jesus would ask…

The Romans are bad and the Jews are good.

Jesus would say that "good" and "bad" mean very different things in different mouths. He doesn't judge people. He says no one asked to be who they are… nothing… no man, no animal, no tree, no flower.

Mary, I think he is dangerous. You must be careful.

Men who are different are dangerous.

Not this man.

Are you sure?

Is one ever sure? But Jesus is like no man I have ever met. I think I love him.

The old man was listening in his corner of the room. The two women had thought he was asleep. It was now totally dark outside. A small candle was burning on the table. The old man spoke: *I have been listening to you. How can a man who is gentle with a beautiful young woman like Mary be dangerous? As I lay dying, I too often wonder if there is a god. How could there be so much suffering if there was an almighty god? Why would God let people be killed by diseases and wars and be left to suffer in their death beds?*

The woman replied: *God punishes those who are evil.*

Have I been evil? I have never tried to harm anyone in my life. Yet I am suffering every minute of every day. Why doesn't God punish the Romans who steal our money and conquer our land?

God's ways are not man's ways.

How do you know?

The rabbis teach it.

Why do the rabbis know? People follow the rabbis because they have to follow somebody. The rabbis follow other rabbis. Nobody knows if what the rabbis say is true. But nobody dares say what they teach is false. Mary's friend Jesus sounds as though he is not a follower. He is not somebody's sheep.

Mary spoke softly: *No, he isn't.*

I would like to meet him and talk to him. Could you bring him here one day before I die?

Surely. I will ask him tomorrow. We are meeting again in the olive orchard.

Be careful Mary, the woman said. *He could be dangerous.*

X

Just imagine, no one really knows what language Jesus spoke. If you comb through history books, there is no consensus as to whether Jesus spoke Aramaic, Latin, Hebrew, or even a little Greek. In any case, languages come and go and get transformed. In the end, they are only sounds humans make. We have a tendency to think they reveal truth or falsehood. But do they? Jesus thought languages simplify everything. They take the great mystery of life and try to give it sense, meaning, and make it understandable. Jesus knew man would never understand. He used language like he walked: delicately, trying not to kill or damage things underfoot.

For our purposes, it doesn't matter what

language Jesus and Mary spoke together. In the end, what they really created was their own language, a language of a love, the kind that has rarely existed on the face of the earth.

XI

Good morning Jesus.

How are you Mary?

Seeing you in the cool of the Sabbath morning is beautiful. I love the morning when the sun appears again. In the middle of the night, I often fear the sun will take a different path… run away and never come back and we will live in eternal darkness. I've had many dreams about this.

The sun is the earth's dearest friend. Neither will abandon the other.

You know Sabbath is the only morning I can see you because all the other mornings have me tending to the old man. Today his daughter's taking care of him as there's no market for her to go to.

Yes, I know. You've told me. It's why I'll start loving

the Sabbath again.

You don't like the Sabbath, Jesus?

My dear Mary, why should the Sabbath be any different from any other day? If there is a god that deserves our worship, we should be thankful to Him every minute of every day. Why do the priests choose just one day a week where everyone pretends they are righteous? And I hate all this talk about Heaven and Hell and the hereafter. The Kingdom of God should be here and now… on this earth… every moment we are alive.

Yes.

And I have come to dislike all the priests and rabbis that talk about good and evil and sin and salvation. No man has the right to judge another man. Only an all-knowing god could be in a position to judge.

I think the priests judge others so that they can feel good about themselves. They must call others sinners so they can call themselves righteous.

I love your voice, Mary, and what you say. I stopped going to the synagogue years ago. I would ask questions like "How do you know this or that is true?" and they would tell me to fast and pray and I would know. Well, I fasted and I prayed and nothing happened. They would say I hadn't fasted and prayed enough.

What precisely did you ask Jesus? I have had many questions, but I never dared ask them.

Many people have questions that they don't dare ask. They are afraid of the priests. I am afraid of no priest.

So tell me about your questions… before I kiss you.

Jesus and Mary both laughed. For many days now, Jesus had wanted to kiss Mary, but had not dared to be the one to instigate their first embrace. He knew that many men had thrown themselves upon Mary. He didn't want to be another such man. He wanted their first kiss to come from her.

And it would come in a few minutes. Mary would take Jesus's hand and then their four lips would become one. But first Jesus would talk about his questions.

I had dozens and dozens of questions, Mary. They started filling my head when I was twelve or thirteen years old. Questions like: If God created the earth, who created God? Why do the Romans and Greeks have many gods and the Jews only one? When we pray, how do we know God is listening? Why would God allow so much suffering? How do we know that the thoughts that fill our heads correspond to the truth of the world...? And then I would look at the sky and wonder: Is our world really the center of the universe like the rabbis say? What... what is out there in that deep blue sky? Nothing? Other worlds? Different worlds? Different creatures and different gods? And those stars that fill the sky when the sun disappears... Where do they come from? How far away are they? Do they have wings? Do they fly? Are we flying? If there is a god, what would he or she or it be like? Maybe God is very different from man... maybe God has no interest in man at all... or maybe God created nothing... a shepherd didn't create his sheep... perhaps God is a Shepherd who found men and decided to take care of them... maybe there is no God... maybe man is God but just doesn't know it... maybe man must become God... Oh Mary, I had so many questions passing through my head. The teachers all thought I was crazy.

Jesus had been sitting on the grass. He slowly extended his body and lay flat on his back. He stared at the sky, then closed his eyes. That is when Mary kissed him, at first very gently. But soon they would be rolling in the grass, their lips and bodies powerful magnets.

Minutes went by. When their bodies finally separated, there was a moment of silence until Jesus spoke again.

Mary, what if everything the Jews say is untrue? What if everything the Romans say is untrue? What if no one knows what the truth of the world is? I have tried to pray hundreds of times. I prayed to the Jewish god. I prayed to the Roman gods. I got no answers that I could say were answers. I think any answers I got just came from my own head.

You're an honest man Jesus.

I try to be, but one never knows if one is being honest with oneself or not.

At least you try to be honest.

Maybe honesty isn't even a virtue. Maybe power is the only thing that counts.

But power is certainly not a virtue. The Roman soldiers, the ones who have overpowered me and used my body are not virtuous. They are wild animals.

Maybe all men are wild animals. Maybe women are too… just a different kind of animal. The rabbis all say that God created man in His own image. If they're lying, then in whose image was he created?

Maybe he was not created.

I have thought that so many times. At first the thought was a frightening one. It's hard to imagine mankind with no link to a god. But it is possible, Mary. As I look at all the suffering and stupidity in the world, I begin to believe that it is truly possible. Sometimes everything looks so strange and barbaric.

But there are beautiful things too.

Like you.

Like flowers and butterflies and some of the fish in the sea.

Mary and Jesus lay silent again. They touched and kissed again. Both felt like they had never felt before. Jesus had lain with other women many times, but none had ever felt like Mary and he had never felt as he now did in Mary's arms. Mary felt her body tingle and parts of her seemed like they were melting, stone to liquid.

But they did not make love on this day. They would talk some more and make love for the first time another day.

I have often asked the gods what the purpose of life is. How should a man spend his time on earth? But most people are slaves. These questions mean nothing to them, just like they mean nothing to animals. The donkey that carries goods to the market doesn't think about what the purpose of his life should be. That purpose is imposed by his master. It is the same for most people. They do what the rich and the Romans say. They have no time to think about anything except working, eating, drinking, and sleeping. It's not their fault that they haven't time to think. I have been lucky. I've had time to think. But is thinking necessarily good? Maybe thinking makes a person crazy.

You're not crazy Jesus. You're not like the man who cries and rolls in the street.

Maybe every head is different. But most heads don't ask a lot of questions. Most heads are satisfied with very simple answers. They accept what they are told by whoever is in power. They accept what the rabbis and the Romans say. They accept the traditions they are born into. They follow the herd like sheep. But I could never do that. Even as a boy.

Mary rubbed Jesus's chest with her hand. He stared at the sky with brown wide-open eyes. She kissed his neck, then spoke.

Jesus, how much have you thought about the word "love"?

Enough to know what it isn't.

Enough to define it?

I imagine everyone's definition would be a little different.

How does one know if one loves another person?

One doesn't know. One feels it.

Can we trust what we feel?

What else is there to trust?

Do you think animals love each other?

I don't know, but I love animals.

Most animals die too quickly.

Who is to say what is long and what is short?

A minute can be long and a year can be short.

That is one of the mysteries.

They both looked at the sky while the sky looked at them.

Do you think there are any answers, Jesus?

There are more answers than there are questions. But most questions are badly phrased and most answers are empty and learned by rote. The world is such a mysterious place.

Not when we're in each other's arms.
Maybe that is when it is most mysterious, Mary.

They both laughed and rolled in the grass. This time Mary had brought some olives and bread and a few pieces of fruit. Jesus had the jug of wine.

Before going home Mary asked Jesus when he might be able to come and see the old man. He said he would come the next morning when she was caring for him.

XII

The old man's eyes opened when he heard Jesus walk into the room. He tried to sit up in his bed of straw. Jesus motioned for him to stay calm, pushed a stool to the side of the bed and sat down. Mary went outside.

Mary has spoken about you often, Jesus. Thank you for coming.

And she has told me about you. I wanted to meet you.

I am a dying man, Jesus. I will soon be gone. What do you think happens when a person dies?

I'll be honest. I have no idea. Life and death are both mysteries. I'm not even convinced that life and death are opposites.

What do you mean?

I'm not sure if life is one thing and death is another. Maybe all things are tied together.

The rabbis speak of Heaven and Hell. Do you think there is a heaven… and a hell filled with fire and damnation?

The rabbis have no idea. No one has any idea. No dead man has ever returned to the land of the living.

But the rabbis have their sacred books…

How do we know they are sacred? The Romans have their sacred books too. But are they sacred? If one is sacred, the other is not.

Yes… (The old man hesitated. It was difficult for him to speak.) *Jesus, I want to ask you about a dream I once had. I want to tell you about it and then have you tell me what you think.*

Let me hear your dream.

I will try to describe it as clearly as possible… I was in my mother's womb with my twin brother.

Did you have a twin brother?

Yes, but he died shortly after we were born… We were together in the womb. Our world was dark and liquid like that of fish in the bottom of the sea. I said to my brother, "Do you think there is life after we leave this womb?" "No," he said. "This is all there is…" And then we were born. We breathed our first breaths of air. We saw our mother. We saw light and the sky. We sucked our mother's breast. There was life after the womb. Then my brother died. I asked my mother, "Mother, do you think there is life after this life on earth?" And in my dream my mother answered, "No, this is all there is!" And then I woke up.

It is a beautiful dream.

But what do you make of it, Jesus?

Maybe your mother was wrong just like your brother was wrong. There was life after the womb. Maybe there is life after our time on earth. Anything is possible. What do you think?

Sometimes I think that maybe life is no different than a dream.

The old man's eyes were drooping. He went on. *You go to sleep, you wake up. You die, you wake up. But where, Jesus? Where do dead men wake up…? I can feel life being sucked out of me… I am being sucked into the tunnel of death… What is on the other side?*

Jesus answered calmly.

No one knows. But the most important thing is that you have lived. You have had this life. One must always appreciate the blessing of being alive.

Sometimes – when I have suffered or have watched others suffer – I have thought life is more of a curse than a blessing.

I can understand that thought. I have had it too. Do you sometimes wish you had died with your brother? The old man hesitated.

Sometimes.

I suspect that at one time or another everyone thinks that life is not worth living. Even kings and princes. Maybe even God.

Yes...

But tell me, my dear friend... Have you ever felt great joy?

Yes... once ... twice... a few times.

And didn't one moment of supreme joy make it all worthwhile?

That is possible Jesus...

As he said this, the old man's eyes closed. Jesus took his hand, bent forward, and kissed it. As he was about to set the hand back on the old man's chest, he felt it turning cold. He held it gently – between his two warm hands – as the old man's head fell to the side.

XIII

The woman did not need her anymore, so Mary came to live with Jesus.

XIV

The sunlight entered through the slits in the walls. Jesus rolled close to Mary and began licking her breast. With her hand, Mary slid the nipple into Jesus's mouth.

You are my son, my lover, and my father. You are all men to me. I never had a father and I have never had a son. I have had many lovers, but none like you. You will be my last lover, Jesus. You are the only lover I have ever loved.

Jesus moved his body, licked between the two breasts and began sucking the other one.

No man has made me feel like you make me feel.

This night I dreamed you were my husband.

I am your husband, Jesus said. *We don't need the rabbis to pronounce us husband and wife. Why should they have the power to do that? Only you and I know how much we love each other. Only you and I can decide our marriage.*

In that case, we've been married since the first time we talked in the olive grove. Since that moment I have never wanted another man.

Nor I another woman.

Jesus's lips left Mary's breasts and found her face in the half light. His hands crawled across her body.

I didn't know I could feel this way about another human being.

I didn't either, Mary. I had never known what it was to truly love someone.

Do you think many people experience such a feeling?

I don't know, but I don't think so. I love every inch of your body and every thought in your head. I have never felt that way before about a woman.

Nor I about a man. How do such things happen?

Love is a mystery. Maybe a greater mystery than life.

When their bodies locked together, they weren't making love… they *were* love.

Jesus and Mary discovered that you cannot truly make love unless you are truly in love. Sex was all over the earth. Love was in their bed.

For a while Jesus began working more. He built more chairs and tables. He built cupboards and beds. He had a friend named Peter who cut down trees and brought him long pieces of fine wood. Sometimes Mary helped Jesus with little details like making the wood smoother so that no slivers would find their way into people's skin. Otherwise, she cooked and made the house comfortable.

In the evening before the sun disappeared they went for walks and talked about the world…

Does anyone know how big it is?

The Romans come from Rome. It takes months to walk from Rome.

Which way is it?

Jesus pointed in the direction of the sinking sun.

That way, I think, though I'm not sure.

Why do the Romans leave their homes to come here?

Why do birds fly from tree to tree? Maybe it is better here. Maybe their king wants to control the world.

Why would anyone want to control the world?

Why would anyone want to control anything? What is it in man that desires power... power over anything... over children, over animals, over a lover, over a population, over land... even over oneself? This is also a great mystery. From where does the urge to dominate come? Some creatures seek to dominate more than others. The Jewish god is said to have power over all of Heaven and Earth. Did He seek that power? The Roman gods fight each other for power. Perhaps man creates gods in his own image... hungry for domination and power. But it's interesting that the Jews don't try to conquer like the Romans. Maybe it's because the Jews have only the one God Almighty who already has all the power. The Roman gods continue their struggle for power; the Roman people continue to try to conquer.

The Romans want power on Earth. The Jews want power in Heaven.

I love your mind Mary.

Where did my mind come from?

It is so different from other minds.

Where does anything come from? It is you, Jesus, who has taught me to appreciate the mystery of all things. Now when I walk about the town, everything has become a matter of wonder – even plants and animals. I look at dogs. Some never bark; others bark incessantly. I observe plants. Some grow tall and spread and climb. Others stay small and take up little space.

It is the nature of nature.

The other day I watched a caterpillar climb up a wall. Where is it going? *I wondered.* Does it have a reason for going where it is going? What is pushing it onward? *Then I asked the same questions as I watched the people of the village.*

That is another great question. What is the motor behind all human actions? Behind all actions? Is there one great motor or are there many small motors?

They held each other's hand as they walked. The touch of fingers can be like making love.

The rabbis say God is the motor.

And if the god the rabbis talk about doesn't exist, then what is behind everything? And even if there is a god, what is the motor behind Him?

Jesus, I love how behind every question you see ten other questions.

Maybe it is better to ask no questions… or at least few questions.

That is what most people do.

And I think animals ask no questions. They just live…

And die.

And as they live and die they don't ask where they are going and where they came from. Only people ask these questions and they accept the first answers that are thrown in front of their faces. The Jews accept the answers the rabbis give. The Romans accept the answers their priests give.

And you Jesus, you accept no answers.

Jesus was quiet for a long moment. *The longer I live the closer I feel to the animals.*

But you just said animals don't ask questions.

Maybe animals don't ask questions because they know there are no answers.

Mary put her arm around Jesus's waist. He put his hand on her far shoulder. Both felt light as clouds.

I often wonder who or what is satisfied being what it is. Are people ever satisfied with who they are and what they have? Are animals satisfied? Are the moon and the sun happy being what they are? Are rocks and rivers and mountains?

Rivers go dry or overflow. Mountains explode or fall. Rocks crack and break.

Not all do.

We don't live long enough to know that.

Do you think that everything is always changing?

That is a thought that has often made me dizzy. So has the thought that the world cannot be stopped… that it is going where it's going and nothing can change its course.

Not even man?

Man is part of its course.

And God?

No one knows if there is a god. And even if God exists, maybe He is also just part of the course.

Jesus, does anyone else think like you do?

I don't know. I don't know anyone else who does. Maybe there are millions of people who think like me in some part of this world or in other worlds. Maybe there are thousands of worlds out there beyond the blue sky of day and the black sky of night. Maybe there are millions of creatures that think like me. I don't know. I don't even know where my thinking comes from. It just happens.

I love your thinking.

And I love yours, Mary. That is one thing I know.

Maybe the only question one can answer in this world is "Whom do I love?"

Maybe love is the only thing that has a core, a centre, a heart. Maybe all the rest is in flux like the river and the wind.

Maybe love is the only thing that is eternal.

It might be eternal, but it is also the rarest of all diamonds.

Jesus and Mary stopped and kissed on the path where they were walking. Their bodies locked like pieces of an intricate puzzle. When their lips finally separated Jesus whispered:

I am getting hungry.

You are always hungry.

For you my darling.

I made a new kind of bread today. It has dried grapes in it.

Then let's go home and feast.

XVI

Here is what Jesus thought as he worked the following morning making a table for the Roman captain who knew that if he asked Jesus to make something it would get made.

When I'm near Mary, I feel as if my whole body is pulled toward hers. It is as if I am inside her and she is inside me. Is it possible that two humans can actually blend together, melt together, truly experience "living" together? I had always felt so alone in this world. Of course, I am friendly with all the people I meet – at least I try to be as I never want to make life worse for any creature – but until I met Mary, I had never had anybody I could share and exchange everything with. It is as if our guts and brains have been mixed together

*and have been put into one body… love's body…
Sometimes Mary gets worried and thinks I don't love
her and that I care about other women. Sometimes I
even think the same about her. But such feelings never
last. We both know that there is no other person on
Earth that we can love the way we love each other… I
am fascinated by everything in the world, but I am
most fascinated by the feeling I have for Mary. When
we are together – walking, sitting at the table, in bed,
anywhere – I feel her presence as if she were a bonfire
that constantly heats every part of my body. It is as if
through Mary the whole world has become a warm
and beautiful place instead of a cold ugly place…
What is the world in itself? Nothing. It is only what
we make of it. It is only the human head that decides
what it is… And as every human is different, every
vision of the world is different… With Mary, my
vision has changed. Things that used to have no
meaning are now charged with meaning… a bird, a
cloud, the wind, a piece of bread, the tiniest insect…
everything is fascinating and mysterious… The
explosion of love is an explosion of life… And death?
What is death in all this? If life cannot be eternal, love
must be eternal. Love must conquer death. If there is
no God, one must become God. Tragedy would be if*

death brought an end to our love... I cannot imagine our love ending. I cannot imagine the world ending. The Jews see death as opening the door to Heaven. For them death is not tragic. But does death open anything except a hole in the ground wherein a body is dropped and covered to be eaten by worms? All I know is that this life is precious. It's all we have, like the man who only has one donkey. That donkey becomes everything... Does life only regenerate on Earth? New trees grow. New babies get born... But are the dead dead forever...? All I know is that since I have known Mary, the world has become a diamond, a jewel floating somewhere in the middle of everywhere... of nowhere...

Jesus worked on the table until the sun disappeared for the day. He had promised the Roman captain it would be ready for Saturday, a *feriae imperativae* – a day of celebration. The Romans had many holidays. Sometimes even the slaves were given time to rest. But such things depended on the emperors; some had bigger hearts than others. The emperors were the gods on Earth. They could often be cruel.

XVII

The Roman captain was a most pleasant person. His name was Marcus. When he came with three of his men to pick up the table, Jesus had them sit down at it and offered them all a glass of wine. The soldiers were young, not more than eighteen, but they listened as their boss and Jesus talked.

You have done fine work on the table Jesus. It's good to have a carpenter I can count on.

It's good to have a Roman captain who pays. A few minutes before, the captain had slipped three denarius coins into Jesus's hand.

You've had bad experiences in the past?

A few times. Not just with Romans, but also with Jews and Greeks.

There are good and bad people everywhere.

You would know more than I. I have never travelled far from my home. Tell me Marcus, what are the people like in Rome?

Most are very pleasant, but much depends on the circumstances of their lives. Much, but not everything. There are gentle rich people and there are cruel rich people. Most of the poor are meek, but there are poor people who can murder.

I have spent half of my life trying to figure out why some people are kind and others are cruel.

Have you found an answer?

No, but the more I think about it, the more I believe a human being has no more free will than a dog. Some dogs are kind, others are cruel. Why? Dogs don't "choose" to be kind? They don't "choose" to be cruel. No one would say that. They just turn out the way they are for an infinity of reasons. I think the same is true for men. One cannot blame a man for being a fool. One can only blame the world. One should not praise a man for being kind. One should praise the world.

And that is why you don't judge people?

Yes. No one truly knows another person's life. Without knowledge one has no right to judge. And knowledge is never complete. Others have no right to judge me, so I don't judge them. No one knows my life and I know no one else's life.

I agree with you, Jesus.

Friends tend to think alike.

What fascinates me is how some people always have power over others. And whoever has power judges and decides what is right and wrong, good and bad. Power always thinks it has the right answers.

You're a wise Roman captain, Marcus. Have some more wine.

Thank you.

And your men, too.

They are barely men, but they serve me well.

They must drink.

And I must ask you a question. I have heard it said that you, Jesus of Nazareth, think that you are a god. Is that true?

Jesus laughed. *That is a perfect example of how stupid people are. I don't blame them for their stupidity, but that doesn't take it away... Marcus, nothing is farther from the truth. It is true that I don't believe in the Jewish god or the Roman gods. I see no proof for any gods. I look at the world and have no idea where it came from, where it's headed or why we are here. When I say "we", I mean everything – animals, plants, rocks, the sun, the moon. It is also true that I have said that if there is no God, man must become God. But that is a play on words. I have no idea what a "god" might be. I think all the gods I have heard about are simply inventions of the human mind. A "real" god might be something totally different, something that no man could possibly understand. When I say man must become God, all I mean is that man must try to become better. He must try to be less stupid, less cruel, less flat-headed… less of what I see him to be today. But of course, maybe that's impossible. Maybe man can never be other than what he is.*

Do you prefer the Jewish god or the Roman gods?

The young soldiers drank their wine and looked intently at Jesus. They had never heard such a conversation before.

I have no preference. I think both are rather odd. The Jewish god can be cruel and seems to seek constant adoration. Tell me, Marcus, why would a god want people to pray to him constantly? Why would a god want to be "worshipped"? Men who want to be worshipped look silly to me. They are weak. They are unsure of themselves. A strong man does not need other people to tell him he is such.

And the Roman gods? Do you like them better than the Jewish god?

They are droll. They are just like people. They play and fight and love and hate. They get offended and they seek revenge. They are not "god-like"… they are "people-like."

And so what would a god be like, Jesus?

I have no idea Marcus. None. Zero. That is part of the great mystery of existence. But I just look at the suffering, death, and the horrors of the world and wonder why.

Why what?

Why wars are fought… why people get sick and die… why criminals steal and kill… why women are raped… why people are nailed to wooden crosses and left to die… why children are whipped… Sometimes I think man is the worst animal on earth. Only men kill each other without the intention of eating. Animals don't do this. They only kill to eat… to survive. Men kill animals to eat and they kill each other because they are stupid. I often think the words "man" and "animal" are very wrong and misunderstood. Often man is more "animal" than the animals and animals are more "man" than men.

You're right Jesus. I myself often look at birds and think they are the greatest creatures on earth. No man can fly through the sky.

Yes Marcus. Birds are so beautiful and skilled.

Have you ever seen a lion or a tiger?

No, but I have heard about them.

They too are amazing. Like horses, they can run much faster than men. They can kill a man with great ease.

But do they kill for stupid reasons?

They only kill when they are hungry or feel endangered.

Men kill men for land and power and foolish ideas about justice and religion.

And that is why you say man must try to become God?

That is why I say man must try to become better than he is.

But can he?

I have my doubts. We can only try.

Who is "we", Jesus?

You… me… anybody who thinks like we do.

Most men don't think like we do.

Most men don't think; they follow.

There was a silence around the table now in Jesus's house. Jesus poured more wine for everybody. Finally Marcus spoke again.

I think we must be going Jesus. We must prepare things for tomorrow's festival.

Every day should be a festival… even days when we work. From birth to death life should be a celebration.

Thank you for the table.

It's my pleasure to work for you.

Before leaving the captain added: *I see a woman's robe over there on the bed. Do you have a wife now, Jesus?*

I have a woman, not a wife. And I love her more than anything on earth.

You are very lucky Jesus.

We are very lucky.

The Romans picked up the table and were gone.

XVIII

Mary kissed Jesus and then stared at the ceiling. They had been locked together in love for half an hour and now were resting. Jesus looked at Mary's face.

Mary, if there is a god in Heaven who decides to judge me positively when I die and says to me, 'Jesus, what I liked about you was that you were an honest man and tried to be good to other creatures. Even though you doubted me, I am still going to let you stay with me in Heaven. Had I been in your place, I probably would have doubted me too... So, I have decided to let you draw the woman you want to spend eternity with. Show me exactly the woman you want and I will create her for you...' Mary, I would draw you. Exactly as I see you now. Everything. Your eyes, nose, mouth, arms, legs, breasts, shoulders, hair, teeth, feet, hands… exactly like you are. That is how much I love you. And then if God said, 'Tell me what kind of brain you want in the head of this woman,' I would tell him about your brain and I would have it all too. That is how much I love you.

And Mary was filled with joy and she said to Jesus, *And I will say the same thing to God about you.*

Jesus's right eye became teary and soon they were locked again together in love. If there is an all-seeing eternal God, He looked down on them and witnessed what true love is, the fusion of two bodies into one. No separation. No me here and you there. If it didn't happen with Adam and Eve, it was happening with Jesus and Mary.

And when they finally unlocked and lay side by side on the bed of straw, Mary said, *I know what Heaven feels like.*

What? Jesus asked.

Orgasm.

They both laughed and wondered if it could possibly be true.

Darkness was coming to the world. Mary rose

from the bed and went outside to pee. Jesus prepared the table with plates, bread, olives, and wine. Mary returned and they supped in candlelight.

They slept until the sun returned, waking only once for Jesus to pee before returning them both to Mary's idea of paradise.

XIX

Mary had risen early and gone to the market. Love had flown her through the night and when she walked she felt like her arms were the wings of an angel. She didn't know life could feel so good. She didn't walk; she danced. She didn't think; her mind was a flowerbed. She didn't go to the market alone; Jesus was in her soul…

Speaking of souls, Jesus lay in bed wondering what a soul might be. People talked about souls and bodies as if one was as real as the other. His body he could touch. He lived inside of it. He was it. But his soul? What was that? Maybe he did not live inside his body. Maybe he was only body. Then he wondered about his thoughts… all people's thoughts… Where do they come from? Do they come from the mind or are they the mind? Is the mind the soul? When the Jews pray to God are they really just praying to their own minds? Are their souls simply talking to themselves? Is thinking a bodily process like peeing? Is peeing a spiritual process like thinking? Are spirit and soul the same thing? Or are they the same no thing… the same nothing? The priests talk about the spirit of man and the spirit of God as if they were as tangible as bread and olives. But what are they…? Really?

Then Jesus wondered where the world came from. He had learned the word "cosmology" when he was a boy. It came from the Greeks who liked to think about the cosmos. Jesus couldn't help thinking about the cosmos. He couldn't help thinking about the biggest things and the smallest things. He couldn't help thinking about causality, about what caused what. Did God cause everything? What caused God? The Jews had their answers. The Romans had their answers. The Greeks had other answers, similar to the Roman answers and very different from the Jews. That allowed for only three possibilities. Maybe there were others. Maybe there were other parts of the earth where people had very different ideas about where everything came from and where everything was going…

Jesus couldn't help being Jesus. He couldn't help being inquisitive. He couldn't accept simple answers to the most profound questions. Sometimes he wondered if maybe there were no answers to the profound questions. The more Jesus thought about things, the less he knew about things. The priests had simple answers for everything. They took the answers that their fathers had taken and their fathers' fathers had taken. The Romans did the same. The Greeks did the same. Jesus could not be satisfied with his fathers' answers.

Sometimes when he thought these kinds of thoughts, Jesus was full of fear and trembling. Sometimes his head would feel like it was going to explode, and he would feel so alone. But this morning when he thought these thoughts of cosmology, he felt no fear and his body didn't tremble once. Why? Because he had just spent the most beautiful night with Mary. And the day with Mary had been beautiful. And the day and the night before had been beautiful… Since he had met Mary, his feelings about everything had changed. Where there had been darkness, now there was light. Where there had been fear, now there was comfort. Where there had been ugliness, now there was beauty. Where there had been hate, now there was love. Where there had been death, now there was life…

With these thoughts in his mind, Jesus began to think about how some people (and animals too – for Jesus was a lover of birds and four-legged creatures and even creatures with no legs) could be in such horrible situations and others could be in such wonderful situations… People in the same world, in the same town, even in the same family. A woman here could be so happy and in such good health. A woman there could be so sad and sick and suffering. How? Why? Who or what was to blame? Was the person to blame? Was the world to blame? Was life to blame? Was God to blame? And what if nothing was to blame? Or everything?

Here as Jesus lay in bed with the smell of Mary on his fingers, he had a thought that very few men have, a thought that would colour his life forever: What if everything that existed was totally innocent? What if nothing that existed was responsible for being what it was? What if everything in all cosmology was not "caused", but just "was"? Or what if all causes were tied together and could not be separated? Didn't both amount to the same thing…? That nothing was to blame… Or everything was to blame… but then "blame" was the wrong word. A better word would be "responsible"… everything was responsible for everything else… But that was not true either… No, nothing was responsible. Everything just *was*. Everything was like a newborn baby. No baby asked to be born. No baby asked to have the parents it had. No tree asked to be planted. No cloud asked to float through the sky. No sun asked to burn in the sky. The sky didn't ask to hold the planets. The planets and moon didn't ask to turn around the earth. Maybe the earth was turning around something it didn't choose too…

Jesus's thoughts then flew from the biggest things to the smallest things… but his ideas were the same. Nothing asked to be what it was. Everything was innocent.

These thoughts might have felt different if he hadn't been so in love with Mary.

Who was Herod? Much has been said and written about him, but did anyone have access to the depths of his heart and head and urinary tract? Did he ever love anyone? Did anyone ever love him? It is said he had eleven wives. Were they all forced to marry him? Did any marry for love? Did all marry with an eye on wealth and power? Does anyone know the secrets of his wives' lives? Why does anybody end up marrying anybody else? What infinity of circumstances brings any two people together? How could Herod build such a beautiful temple when he was such a bad man who would kill his own wives and children? What made Herod be Herod? Even Herod didn't know.

What motor propels one man to kill, conquer,

and enslave and another man to wander in the desert and contemplate the beauty of a flower? One generation produces Herod. The next produces Jesus.

The Jews say they are children of God. Whose god? Which god? Did God not want women to read and write? Maybe that was not such a bad thing, for what would women have been reading? The Bible? An eyeful of lies about the history of the world?

What can be said of a world full of so many slaves? What can be said of a world filled with so much suffering? What can be said of a world with something so beautiful as the love between Mary and Jesus?

The Jews say the flesh of a pig is unclean and should never be eaten. It is their law. Whence comes this law? Probably from a man who got sick after eating part of a pig a few thousand years ago. The man called himself a prophet. He was full of bad pig and full of dumb shit. But his law has lasted for more than two millennia.

From where do ideas about right and wrong come? Why are the world's laws what they are? What is the origin of good and evil? Are Mary and Jesus committing adultery? Are they sinning? Are they committing love? Are they writing a new Bible?

Aren't all of "God's laws" really just "man's laws?" And aren't they usually conceived of by unhappy men who take their unhappiness out on other people? Don't they simply want others to share their misery? Isn't it because their bodies are sick that they denigrate the flesh? Do they not want others to feel guilty so they can pull them into their mud? Aren't they keen to enslave the minds and flesh of others because they themselves are not strong enough to be free?

For years Jesus listened to the rabbis talk. When he asked such questions they had no answers. Or if they did have answers, they were bad answers. Dead answers. Answers that were not real. Answers with no foundation. They would say things like, "Because it is written in the Torah." And then Jesus would ask, "But why is what is written in the Torah true?" And they would say, "Because it is the Word of God." And Jesus would ask, "But how do you know it is the Word of God? The Romans and Greeks have different gods. Which god or gods are real? No one has seen God. No one has talked to God. No one really knows anything about God." And when Jesus would say this, the rabbis always looked at him like he was crazy, muttered among themselves about Moses and burning bushes, but without conviction. But he was quite sure that he wasn't the one who was crazy.

The rabbis had no idea why they believed what they believed. Didn't they believe what they believed because their fathers had believed it? Weren't their beliefs based on one thing and one thing only: tradition? They would never answer yes to these questions because to do so would leave them naked, lonely, lost, afraid. They, like most men, were not strong enough to create new values and new reasons to live. So they followed their fathers who had followed their fathers' fathers.

Jesus did not think all this was necessarily bad. He simply thought it was human. Humans were weak. Even Herod was at bottom weak. Doesn't one who kills his wives and sons do so because he himself is weak?

The Bible of the Jews says, "Thou shalt not kill." But the Bible doesn't mean that thou shalt never kill. It means, "Thou shalt not kill except when God tells thee to kill," which historically was quite often. God tells thee to kill when people are "wicked" and don't believe in Him…

So Jesus would say to the rabbis, "But if people have different gods and these different gods all say that it is okay to kill people who don't believe in their god, then we have war. Isn't war bad?" And the rabbis would say that there was only one true god and that true god was their God. And Jesus would point out that the other side thought their god was the true god. But the rabbis would dismiss him as a fool or a troublemaker…

So Jesus began to think that it was all a circus. But whose fault was it? Was it a man's fault if he was too weak to believe in anything except the traditions of his fathers? Was it a man's fault if he was jealous or stupid? People can't help themselves. People can't be other than they are. People don't understand who they are and why they do what they do.

Jesus thought about these things. He eventually stopped talking to the rabbis.

Seasons passed. Years passed. "Can one know the truth?" Jesus began to wonder. "Probably not," he thought. "But maybe one can know what the lies are."

Jesus tried diligently to respect other people and their beliefs. But if these other people didn't respect each other or didn't respect him, then what was he to do? If these others said that he and Mary were adulterous sinners and wanted to kill Mary, then what should he do? Stand and watch? If they wanted to kill him, what should he do? Let them? Jesus wouldn't blame them because he knew that they could be nothing other than what they were. "Blame" was not part of Jesus's vocabulary. But were there not limits to what one could tolerate?

Little by little Jesus began to see life as a kind of jungle, as a savage place. He saw that the only thing that ruled the world was power. Herod had had power. Now his son had power. Pontius Pilate had power. Some of the rabbis had power. Power moved from one person to another, from one group to another. Laws were made by those who had power. Slaves had no power. Women had no power. They never said who should do what. They never made the rules.

Jesus wondered what was good and what was bad. He realised that what was good for one was often bad for another. What was good for the Romans was bad for the Jews and vice versa. Perhaps the world was not a moral place. Could it be made better? Could the slaves be freed? Could women one day share the power? Would there ever be "goodness" and "truth" on Earth?

Jesus did not know. But of one thing he was quite certain: all the talk he had heard about Heaven and Hell and another world after death was probably a pack of lies. He had never seen any dead man come back to life. Never… Did that mean there was nothing after death and nothing before birth? Of course, he didn't know. No one knew. But he and everyone else did know that there was a here and a now. Why did people ignore this life and talk about an "afterlife?" This was the real sin. The Kingdom of God – if there was one – was here and now. It had to be. That was the only thing that made sense. This life must be cherished. This life must be loved and respected. The odds were that this life was all there was…

Thus thought Jesus one summer day in the part of the world called Palestine.

XXI

When Mary and Jesus made love together they were both amazed that the feeling was so different from when they had made love with other people before. With others Jesus had never felt like he could make love forever. With others Mary had never felt her flesh heat up until it eventually melted into the other's body. With each other, Mary and Jesus became one. Each totally loved the other. They loved the self. The self became the other. The other became the self.

When this kind of feeling is present you cease to make love; you become love. There's no geometry or mathematical calculation because there's no separation. There aren't two bodies interacting because there's only one body loving. There's no you and I; there's only we.

Jesus and Mary wondered how many people in the world had a chance to feel the way they felt. They imagined very few. An infinity of circumstances had been necessary to bring them together. It would take another infinity to pull them apart.

XXII

How often is a human being able to climb out of his or her box? Here of course we're talking about the mental box… the box of thinking, language, values, beliefs… The Greeks and Romans thought many things about cosmology. They often did not agree with each other. Parmenides, Anaxagoras, Epicurus, Aristotle, Ptolemy, Empedocles, Plutarch, Zeno, Cicero, and many others had ideas about where everything came from, what it was made of, and how it worked. There was little consensus. Jewish cosmology was monolithic. Everyone agreed. The Jews stapled themselves to the Biblical cosmology which seems to have been based on old Babylonian ideas: the earth and the heavens form a unit within the "infinite waters of chaos"… the earth is flat and circular and a solid dome – "the firmament" – keeps out the chaos. And, of course, there was the story of one God, Jehovah, creating everything in six days, then taking a much-deserved rest. Eventually Christianity and Islam bought into the Jewish cosmology and pounded it into the head of the Western world until Copernicus and Galileo came along. But they were forced to shut up and it took a few more centuries before any real climbing out of the Jewish-Christian-Islamic box was possible. And only a small group of people were able to do it. Most people's minds are still today deeply coloured by the old Jewish vision of God creating the world, man being "free," and Hell waiting to suck up the sinners after death and Heaven opening its doors to the good.

Take a few minutes one clear summer day and lie on your back in a field or on a park bench and look at the sky. I don't say look "up" at the sky because the odds are there is no "up" or "down" in the universe. When you look at the sky imagine all the explanations we have for everything. But there is an immediate problem: we don't really have any idea what "everything" is. Sure, we have our box of

21st century science and the universe being around for 13,000,000,000 years and the "big-bang" and all that. But isn't that too a residue of the old Babylonian idea of "a creation" and time being linear. What about the mystery, the great mystery of it all? And just imagine, as hard as it tries and as profound as it thinks itself to be, maybe the human mind can never really know…

If you look at the sky long enough and let your mind fly far enough and put all preconceived ideas in parentheses, you will eventually start to get dizzy. The deep deep mystery will hit you. All cosmologies will look feeble, like paltry endeavours of the human head to explain things. When you finally stand up again, if you are weak you will depart with heavy feet and go bury yourself in the nearest safe dark cave… say a newspaper, or a TV, or a church. If you are strong you will dance toward nowhere with light feet, your head high, and your nose pointed toward the sun.

XXIII

When Jesus finally stood up he felt light-headed. He didn't know how long he had been lying in the grass on the hill in the olive grove. No watches or clocks in the Holy Land. Only the sun and shadows to tell the time and because the sun was fat and low, he imagined Mary would be waiting for him.

She was.

Where did you go?

I went up to the olive grove where we first walked together. I lay down and looked at the sky.

And what did you see?

Your face on a big blue wall. But first I thought about everything I could think about.

You think too much Jesus.

Do you think so my darling?

Where can all this thinking take you? It is always a dead end.

Maybe so, but let me tell you what I thought.

Of course. If nothing else, I love the sound of your voice.

And I love yours… I thought about all the things that I've been told my whole life through. I thought about what my parents told me and what the rabbis tried to drill into my head. I thought about what my Roman friend Marcus told me about how the Romans see the world. I thought about what my friends John, Paul, Matthew and Mark think about everything. And then I stared at the blue sky and wondered if it was a ceiling like the Jews say or an infinity like some of the Greeks and Romans say.

And which did you vote for?

I didn't vote. I tried to think of other possibilities.

That is so you, Jesus. Mary laughed, but lovingly so. *You always see the complexity of everything.*

I can see nothing else. Things are deep. Time is deep. Space is deep. Every tree, flower, donkey, and man is deep. But the human mind is shallow. Too readily satisfied with simple answers, answers like the rabbis give.

Yes, if there is one thing I have learned from you, Jesus, it is that.

And what is the deepest thing of all, my love?

I've learned that too. But only because I feel it, not because I think it.

Feeling is everything.

And that is why love is the deepest thing of all. It is love that is felt the deepest.

And that is why when I looked at the sky, I saw your face. I see you everywhere. I feel you everywhere.

And what is felt the deepest is also perhaps the greatest mystery.

Everything is a mystery.

Not to shallow minds.

To shallow minds everything can be explained.

Why would anyone want to explain the feeling I have for you?

I don't know, Jesus said.

Mary and Jesus moved closer and closer to each other. And Jesus moved closer to an absurd crucifixion.

XXIV

Good morning Marcus.

Good morning Jesus.

What are you doing here so early?

I want to talk to you, to warn you.

To warn me about what? Is war approaching? Someone invading?

No, it's secure. We have almost all the world under our control.

Exactly how big is the world?

We don't know for sure. We haven't seen it all. No one has walked and walked without eventually turning back.

I have walked for three days in every direction. That is what I have seen.

And I have ridden a horse for a hundred days to get

here. That is what I have seen.

So what is it you want to warn me about, Marcus my friend?

People are talking about you Jesus. Both Romans and Jews. Some of my officers are saying you are beginning to disturb the peace in Palestine. And the rabbis say you are blaspheming God.

How can I be disturbing the peace when I have never injured a man or an animal in my life?

They fear you might incite a revolt.

A revolt? Against whom?

Us. The Romans. Pontius Pilate.

I'm not stupid. Someone will always have power. Your lot aren't bad people. Better Romans have the power than some other crueler people.

I know that's what you think, but they don't.

Well, tell them.

I have no power. They won't listen to me. I'm a lowly captain. Only twenty men under my command.

If you don't want to tell them, I will. I have nothing to hide.

They might come and talk to you soon Jesus. That is what I've heard. They want to hear your ideas firsthand.

Marcus, the only revolt that interests me is the revolt

of a man against himself. One cannot change the world, but one can change oneself.

But maybe you can change the world, Jesus. You have something about you that makes people listen to you.

People might listen, but they don't hear. There are very few people I have talked to who understand me. Even my friends Paul, Mark, John, and Matthew misinterpret what I say.

What do you mean?

They think I am the son of God. Every man is the son of God and every woman is the daughter of God. But those words mean nothing because no one knows who God is or what God might be. We are all really sons and daughters of the earth. But so are donkeys, goats, sheep, serpents, flowers, trees and clouds. My friends cannot escape the idea of the Jewish god. They want me to pretend I am the awaited son. I make no such pretension. No one knows where the earth came from.

If you had been born in Rome, maybe people would have said you were the son of Jupiter.

I don't know. We will never know because I was born here in Bethlehem. A man lives his life only once. All he can try to do is make the best of it… and try to help others have a chance to have a good life along the way.

A good life being…?

Marcus, each man must search his own heart and find his own way. Most men don't search very hard. They simply accept the world and beliefs they are born into. Very few men think for themselves. Very few men wonder and marvel and look behind the surface at the great complexity and mystery of life.

Maybe men are afraid of the mystery and complexity.

Yes, either afraid or incapable of seeing it.

Then it's not their fault.

That's true Marcus. But like water makes a flower grow, I hope my words will make people grow. But there's no guarantee. The majority of men are like sheep. They follow the herd. This isn't so much a bad thing. It's just a necessary thing. And, if a man is a sheep then let him have his shepherd. If he must blindly follow the herd, then so be it.

And you have nothing against the herd, Jesus?

Most people are stuck in the world they are born into, like trees planted in the ground. If the herd followed me in a revolt, they'd still be a herd. When the revolt was over they'd still be sheep. So I'm not interested in followers. Of course, I love all mankind like I love all of the night sky. But I love most the star that shines in the night. I want to see men flying with their own wings. I want to see men take their own road. I want each man to find his own Heaven on Earth.

And what might that heaven be, Jesus?

I can't tell you. You must find it for yourself. I'm not you. I can't prescribe what's good for you. You must discover that yourself. That is why I want no followers. Followers will always be weak. I want to see people grow strong.

You are wise Jesus. You must tell all this to the Roman leaders. They fear you want power over the people.

I want power only over myself. If your leaders come, I will tell them what I think. I will tell them what a great mystery this world is.

For them, life is not a mystery. They only care about their stomachs and their penises.

They are human. I often think I should never expect more of a man than that he cares about his stomach and his penis. One cannot make wine out of water. One cannot make a snail fly. But I can't help trying, Marcus. I can't help dreaming of a heaven on Earth.

No. But you must also take care Jesus. People are misunderstanding your ideas. And power hates to be questioned.

You're quite right. If and when your leaders come, I'll be careful. But I'll be honest. I mean no harm to Roman or Jew.

I'll be going now Jesus. My men are waiting. We're making a road from Nazareth to Bethlehem.

Thank you for coming by Marcus. Goodbye my dear friend.

Goodbye, Jesus.

XXV

When Jesus and Mary made love that night, he thought he was going to disappear into her belly. Not the first time, but the second. The first time he was as strong as a wild bull and he roared as he sent his thick juice into her heart. But the second time, perhaps a half an hour later, he felt like a delicate little mouse scurrying into the hole of its mother and when his juice flew he whimpered softly and flew with it and dissolved in the womb from which he came.

XXVI

The next morning Jesus went looking for his friends, John, Mark, Matthew and Paul. He had known them for many years and they had shared many moments together. Like all friends, sometimes they spent more time together than others. Since Jesus had met Mary, he saw them less.

They were sitting in a shady area in Nazareth's central square.

Where have you been Jesus? Has Mary put a leash around your neck? Have you become a dog?

I have nothing against dogs. Sometimes I think it would be better to be a dog than a man. At least some dogs run free.

Ha! You've said many times that nothing is free.

You're right, John. I have no idea what freedom might be. Maybe a dog on a leash can be freer than a dog running in the wild.

Would you rather be a dog or a donkey, a Roman or a Jew, a man or a woman, a god or a sun?

I would be happy to be any and all of them. Just existing is the greatest gift.

Are you crazy Jesus or are you the son of God, like Paul reckons you say you are?

I never said he was the son of God, John. What I said was that if there was a son of God in Palestine it was Jesus. But I never said there was a son of God in Palestine.

And I would never say I am the son of God, Jesus rejoined, because I have no idea if there is a god. There is no proof of any deity.

The rabbis say we don't need proof; we only need faith.

I know Mark. We heard the rabbis say this a thousand times. But tell me why I should direct my faith in the direction of the Jewish god instead of the Roman gods… or any other god for that matter.

You directed your faith toward Mary…

Mary is real. She walks and talks.

She has a spirit… God is spirit…

What does "spirit" mean? You don't know. I don't know. The rabbis don't know. No one knows.

Why do you doubt everything Jesus?

Because when I was a boy the rabbis said I must seek the truth. I did. And the truth became very complicated. The more I thought, the less truth became evident. Maybe there is no truth.

Do you think the Bible is a lie?

The rabbis just wanted me to believe "their" truth. I have no idea what is true. But I have no proof that the Bible is any truer than the Roman version of the world.

Maybe we should start a religion based on lies.

Maybe all religions are based on lies. Why should we start another one?

Maybe we can start a better world.

The only thing that can make the world better is love.

Then let us start a religion based on love.

Love can only happen between two people. As soon as more than two people are involved, love falls apart. There will never be a religion based on love. Love is a private matter.

The Bible says, "Love thy neighbour as thyself."

That is not a good commandment. Most people do

not love themselves. The Bible says, "Do unto others as you would have them do unto you." This too is a bad idea because most people do not treat themselves well. If you don't know how to treat yourself, how can you expect to know how to treat others?

What are you saying Jesus? That there are no good commandments?

I don't know. But things are more complicated than the rabbis and the Bible make them out to be. For me, the only thing that counts is that every man finds his own road to Heaven. And Heaven must be here on Earth. And at the end of that road there is probably love.

So you and Mary are in Heaven?

Yes. And you can be too. All men can.

All men aren't as lucky as you are Jesus.

All I know is that others cannot make Heaven for you. You must make it yourself. And when you make it with someone you love, it is even better.

So a slave can live a heavenly life…?

Yes, if the slave finds love.

And a king can live a life in hell…?

Yes, if he never finds love. Look at Herod. He had eleven wives and power over all of Palestine, yet his life was hell. No one ever loved him and he never truly loved anyone. Love is the only religion that makes any sense. And any church with more than two people is too big. People who love, see the world as a heaven. People who never love see the world as a hell. It is that simple.

But what about Heaven and Hell in the next world?

Paul, I have never seen the next world. Neither have you. Neither has any rabbi.

But some have had visions.

The kingdom of God is here and now. It is all we know. All men can enter the kingdom. There is no need for a judgment. No man can judge another man.

It is God's job to judge.

And if there is no God?

If there is no God, then the only judges are men.

And men are always bad judges. Men never truly understand the world. They never understand what causes what. When men judge they simply eliminate what they don't like. They punish what they don't agree with. That is not judgment; that is simply the exercising of power.

So what should one do?

Find your own way. Love. Marvel at the mystery of everything around you.

But what if there is no love on my road? What if everything around me is ugly, cruel, and stupid?

Then life is Hell and tragic. To climb out of Hell a man must be very strong. Only a great man can build a new road.

The friends were silent for a while. John had the pitcher of wine. He offered a cup to Jesus, then he filled his other friends' glasses. They drank together, each in his own thoughts.

XXVII

When he was ten, Jesus had helped his father build the door to their house. It was the first real work he had ever done and his father had made him feel proud. When the two Roman soldiers pounded on that door, Jesus knew who was on the other side and why they were there.

Would you like to come in and share some bread and wine?

We have no time for bread and wine. Are you Jesus of Nazareth?

I am called that.

Then you must come with us to see Pontius Pilate.

Why does he want to see me?

That is not our business. He told us to fetch you

immediately. We follow his orders.

I have been very lucky in my life. I have had to follow very few orders. Do you enjoy following the orders of others?

That is not a question we ask ourselves.

Maybe you should.

We are soldiers. Soldiers do what they are told.

That is a strange way to live.

You must come with us.

If I must, I must. But I would rather eat bread and drink wine with you and talk about the mystery of life. Do you feel the wonderful mystery of being alive?

What mystery? We are Roman soldiers. We were born in Rome. We were sent here. We follow the orders of Pontius Pilate.

And one day you will die. And what will you have done with your lives?

We will have been soldiers and will have served the emperor.

Yes. It is a strange world we live in where everybody serves somebody else.

Jesus, you seem to be a kind man, but we really must not linger.

Will I be away long? Mary will worry if so.

That is not our business.

I am sure it isn't.

It was a quite a long walk to the palace where Pontius Pilate ruled. Jesus asked the soldiers many questions. They asked Jesus none.

There were two guards at the entrance. When the trio arrived the doors were opened. Jesus was happy to get out of the heat of day and into a cool building. He was taken to Pontius Pilate's private office. The soldiers stood at the back of the room while Jesus and the ruler talked.

Good morning Jesus of Nazareth. I've been wanting to meet you.

And I wanted to meet you too Pilate.

Please be seated and let's discuss. We'll waste no time with petty talk… My first question is, who do you think you are Jesus?

That is a wonderful question. One of the most wonderful questions a man could be asked.

So answer it.

I can't.

Why not?

Because no man knows who he is. We think we know who we are. We have a name and a place of birth, a family, a language, a religion, a political system. But that tells us nothing about how our minds and bodies function. That tells us nothing about the why and wherefore of our beating hearts, the blood in our veins, and the stream of thoughts blowing through our brains.

It is the thoughts that I'm interested in. Do you think that you are the son of God?

If I thought I was the son of God, which god would I be the son of… the Jewish god Jehovah or one of your many Roman gods?

You're a Jew. You would think yourself to be the son of Jehovah.

You say I'm a Jew because I was born a Jew. But in my head I'm not a Jew. I don't believe in the god Jehovah any more than I believe in the god Jupiter or any other of your Roman gods.

But you believe in a creator of the world?

I have no idea where the world came from. And no one else does either. You Romans have your explanation. The Jews have their explanation. The Greeks have theirs. Why should I believe one explanation over another? I have no proof or reason to believe in a god. For me the world is a great mystery.

Then you do not think you are the son of God?

No.

Do you think you are God?

That is a totally different question.

Why?

Because if there is no god to follow, who should one follow? Should one follow another man or should one follow oneself? That becomes the question. Should you be my god, Pilate? Should a rabbi be my god? Should a philosopher like Aristotle or Heraclitus be my god? Or should I be my own god?

I can see that you have talked with many philosophers.

No, not really. Mostly I've thought for myself. I've observed people and the world and tried to understand the world. I've tried to think about my thinking and the thinking of others.

Thinking can be dangerous, Jesus of Nazareth.

Dangerous to whom?

To you, to me, to everybody.

It is "not thinking" that's dangerous. People accept silly versions of what life is. They accept silly versions of what good and evil are. They accept silly versions of how they should live, how they should spend their time on Earth. Look at all the slaves in the world. Look at your soldiers. They have no life. Their lives are worse than the lives of most dogs or donkeys.

We treat our soldiers very well. They're well fed. We keep them warm in winter.

Yes, but they're slaves to you. They spend their lives following orders. They never think for themselves. They don't possess their own lives. You possess their lives. The only thing they do on their own is rape the women of Palestine.

Don't presume…

Isn't all we think some sort of presumption?

Pontius Pilate said nothing, but Jesus went on.

And look at the lives of most women in this world. The Jews don't let their women read and write. Women have no power. They're slaves to men. They're forced to make love even if they don't want to, not only to your soldiers, but to their husbands. Can you imagine being forced to make love, Pilate, to a woman you didn't like… even hated? Can you imagine that?

I'm asking the questions.

I thought we were having a discussion.

You're a strong man, Jesus. Strong men are dangerous.

To whom? You're a strong man too, Pilate. Are you

dangerous…? No, because you have the power. You only see me as dangerous because I might be a threat to it. But I threaten nobody's power. I want power only over myself.

Admit that's a lie, Jesus! Surely you want men to be free?

I fear men will never be free. Only animals are free… free until they are killed by other animals or trapped and killed or enslaved by men. Man himself was only ever free if and when he was an animal.

You believe that? You believe that man might have once been an animal?

The truth is, I think man has always been an animal… only now he is a different kind of animal. Now he is an enslaved animal. It's possible that he used to be wild, like goats on a mountain, like hawks in the sky. Maybe he used to run free, his eyes only looking out. But now he lives in society. Society enslaves him. Society tells him who he is and how he must act. Society tells him if he is good or evil. The Jews think the Jews good and the Romans evil. The Romans think the Romans good and the Jews evil. Society makes man silly and weak. Society judges man and makes him feel guilty.

Would you prefer a society with no laws, Jesus?

Of course, man must have some laws. But laws should exist only to help man live the best life possible, to make him strong, to make him maximize his time on Earth.

And who should decide what the good life is?

That is the question, Pontius Pilate… Who should decide? You? Me? The rabbis? Each man for himself?

Jesus, I think you overestimate man. Man does not want to be free. He does not want to think for himself. He wants to follow… anybody. The Jews follow their Bible and their rabbis. We Romans follow Roman tradition and Roman law. You, Jesus, maybe you want to be free. But you are not like other men.

I just want everyone to have a chance to live and not be a slave.

That is a dream, Jesus. It is not real. Most men are not interested in freedom. They might say they are, but in the end they will follow somebody – anybody – like donkeys on a rope.

Perhaps you are right, Pilate. But only a free life is worth living.

What you say is dangerous, Jesus. It has the power to disturb the peace in Palestine and all over the kingdom.

All I am saying is that there must be a better world

than this one. We must find it. We must create it. Is what I say wrong?

It is not wrong; it is dangerous.

Do you not agree with me, Pontius Pilate?

Pontius Pilate was not a stupid man. He did not answer Jesus's last question. He simply stared at Jesus for a few long seconds and finally told him he could go. He also told him to be careful.

XXVIII

When Jesus got home Mary was making bread and cooking fresh vegetables. They embraced before they spoke. Their lips were used almost as much for kissing each other as for talking to each other. When their bodies separated, Jesus poured himself a cup of wine and sat at the table. He observed the beauty and grace of Mary's body for the thousandth time. He thought she moved like a deer he had once seen in a valley near a river.

Where did you go, Jesus?
Only where I was forced to go.
What do you mean?
While you were at the market, two soldiers came and took me to see Pontius Pilate.

Being taken to Pontius Pilate is rarely a good thing.

He's not a bad man. He's just doing his job. He's trying to keep order in Palestine.

Some men do their jobs better than others.

His job is perhaps more difficult than other jobs. He has to assuage both Rome and the Jews.

Why do you think the Romans came all the way to Palestine? Why didn't they just stay in Rome? Why would they want the problems that come with governing other lands?

Why indeed. I often think about the nature of power. Power is an odd animal. It is a bit like a vulture, except vultures prey off the dead. Power preys off the dying and the weak. The weak seek the strong. They live off each other symbiotically until the strong get weaker or the weak get stronger. Then power slips from one hand to another.

An ugly struggle.

The nature of nature! Nature can be ugly.

So what did Pilate want?

Jesus laughed.

He wanted to know if I thought I was the son of God. When I told him I had no proof of the existence of any god, he asked me if I thought I was God.

And what did you say?

I said that if there is no God, then one must decide if one should follow another man or one's own conscience.

That is why he thinks you're so dangerous, because he fears you'll follow only yourself. And he fears you'll encourage others to do the same.

That's true, Mary.

He probably fears other men will follow you whether you want it or not, and that you'll end up leading them against Rome.

I'm no leader.

You're a dreamer, Jesus. Men need a dream to follow.

Jesus laughed again.

Touché! Pilate said exactly the same thing. And I agree with both of you. Even rabbis and kings are followers. They too are slaves... slaves to their positions, slaves to their traditions, slaves to their laws.

So what is the point of trying to change anything?

That is the question I ask myself too. But deep inside me there is a burning desire to believe that some men can be free, that some men can create their own better world.

Do you know any free men?

I'm not sure.

Maybe a free man is a myth just like the gods.

You are wise and wonderful Mary. Sometimes I think that the only time I am free is when I'm loving you.

And when is that?

All the time.

Mary laughed.

Maybe love is the only real act of freedom.

Then she thought for a moment.

But maybe love is the greatest form of slavery.

Maybe it's both. Maybe freedom and slavery are the same thing. I am free to choose you, Mary Magdalene, as the one person on this earth that I love. And then, once I have chosen you, I am a slave to my love for you.

Ah, now maybe you are speaking the truth, Jesus…

I'm your slave. I need you, Mary. I need you to make the beauty of this world visible. I need you in order to feel whole. I need you to talk to. Why talk if there is no one to listen and understand? I need you to express my love. Why make love if there is no one to love? Without you, the fantastic ball of love inside me had nowhere to go. It had nothing to do. Before I met you Mary, a huge part of me was asleep. The part I now know to be the best part. Volcano-like, it had lain dormant. And then… with you… it erupted. I became whole. I was myself. The world became beautiful. Every moment there was a reason to live and move forward. The ball of my life was set in motion. Now I feel we are rolling toward infinity… Infinite love.

You know I feel the same Jesus. Love is the sun that lights the world. Love makes the world beautiful. Love lets us fly… Yes, we are slaves to our love. But without our love we are slaves to a world of darkness.

Jesus and Mary felt their loving growing stronger every day. Both sensed that only death could kill it.

XXIX

The next morning Jesus rose with the sun and went for a walk in the square. The world was chirping and chattering; the marketplace was bustling. Jesus saw his friend John arranging the robes he was hoping to sell that day on a table.

Good morning John. Isn't it wonderful that, after sleep, the world is still here?

It's wonderful that you're still here, Jesus.

It's wonderful that the sun is still here to light up the world. Where do you think it goes at night? Why does it not stay in the sky all day?

I don't know. Maybe it has other business. Maybe it has another world to light up. Maybe it sleeps like we do. And the moon… where does it go during the day?

Perhaps the sun and the moon don't like each other. When one comes, the other runs away.

Do they run or do they fly like birds?

I think they float like clouds.

And where do the clouds come from? They are as magical as the moon and sun.

It is all such an incredible mystery... Do you know, John, there is a Greek man who thinks it is the earth that is moving and that the sun is standing still? It is an amazing thought. I have heard some of the wise men in the marketplace talking.

You are the wisest man in the marketplace, Jesus. Your mind is the most open mind I know. Your thoughts begin where the thoughts of others end.

One cannot know from where one's thoughts come. The human head might be the greatest mystery of all. But then what do we know of the head of a bird or a donkey or even the head of the sun? We are so small. We are tiny specks of being in a universe that might go on forever.

But tiny doesn't mean insignificant. Countless times you've said that yourself.

That's true, John. It is a stupid mind that values things based on their size. The small can be big and the big can be small. The first can be last and the last can be first…

How big do you think the sun and moon are?

We cannot know because we don't know how far away they are.

I was talking with Paul yesterday and he thinks they can change size, like a man. They can be fat one day and small another… especially the moon. What do you think, Jesus?

I have often wondered about the size and consistency of the sun and moon. Of course, the sun is sometimes the hybrid colour of fire. Other times it's pure orange or pure yellow, like certain flowers. The moon is almost always the white of one of your fine robes here. It doesn't change colour as much as it changes shape. It is all such a great mystery, John. Where did it all come from? What moves the moon and sun? Do they have wings? Are they the consistency of rocks? But rocks can't fly. Sometimes the sun looks to be made of fire. But fires burn out. How can the sun burn forever? Maybe they're like flowers that come and go with the seasons, except their seasons are daily.

You ask so many questions, Jesus.

Questions are far more interesting than answers. Questions stimulate the mind; answers put it to sleep.

But people want answers.

This is the problem, John. People want answers so badly that they accept any and every answer. They accept the first answer that society gives them. Even Pontius Pilate wants answers. Yesterday two soldiers took me to his palace to talk to him. He wanted to know if I thought I was the son of God.

Jesus, you're a special man. You're noticeably different from other men. Pilate knows this and so he fears you.

I am no more different than one donkey is from another. The only difference between me and other men is that I ask more questions and am rarely satisfied with the answers I hear.

That, yes, and the fact that you love the world more than other men.

I don't know if "love" is the right word. I'm fascinated by it – fascinated by everything that exists. Existence is the greatest mystery of all. Each and every animal, plant, tree, sun, moon, person, sky, rock, and thought is a great wonder to me. I think I would use the word "love" only for the way I feel about Mary. I would use the word wonderment. Wonderment, fascination, respect for all the rest. I respect the right of everything to exist. But even the word "right" is the "wrong" word. Things don't get given "the right" to exist. Who could possibly bestow that…? Who? A god? A god that might not exist itself? Pontius Pilate? A Roman governor who happens to be in power at the moment? Things exist… that's all. Nobody gives them the right to be.

But in the world there are people who kill. Animals kill each other. What gives them the right to destroy life?

That's just it, John… nothing… nothing gives one man the right to kill another or one animal the right to kill another. It's not a matter of rights. Everything's a matter of power. Power is what runs the world. And power is a very strange thing. It comes and goes like the sun. One day it is gentle, one day it kills… just like the sun.

And who gives power to the powerful, Jesus?

Who made the sun hot, John? Probably nobody. Even if God made the sun, it would only beg the further question, who made God? And to that question there is no answer. Finally, in the end, we can only say that existence just "is." There is no explanation for it.

But people are never satisfied with that kind of an answer.

Because, John, people are people. Be they Jews or

Romans or Greeks, they want answers. Any answer is better than no answer. But not for me. And not for you.

But it's difficult to dance in the fog.

No it isn't. Not if one finds a partner to dance with. That's the meaning of love. When one loves another human being, one can live with no answers… Because love is the answer.

The two fell silent. Each was lost in his own thoughts. Finally, John spoke.

Did Pontius Pilate seem angry with you, Jesus?

No, he seemed rather amused with me. I think he enjoyed our conversation.

You must be careful, Jesus.

That is exactly what he said as I started to leave.

Then be careful.

Be careful of whom and what?

Power… The rabbis and the Romans.

Who do you think I should fear the most, John? Our dear rabbis or our Roman conquerors?

That's a good question.

Maybe I should fear thunder and lightning and the earth when it shakes. They too have power.

But they have a different kind of power.
Are you sure, John?

With that question the two friends bade each other farewell and Jesus went walking up the hill towards the olive grove.

There was a rabbi on Pontius Pilate's council. He did not like Jesus of Nazareth. He kissed Pontius Pilate's ass because he wanted to save his neck in this life. He kissed Almighty Jehovah's ass because he wanted to save his neck in the next.

Rabbi, I saw the man Jesus yesterday. He came here to the palace and we talked.

And what did he say, Pontius Pilate, Honorable Ruler of Palestine?

I asked him if he thought he was the son of God. He categorically said he was not the son of God and that he wasn't sure if there was a God.

He said that… (scowls)… That is blasphemy… To deny God is the ultimate blasphemy. The next thing he will deny is your power over him.

He already has. But he did it in a rather gentle way… (the rabbi's face has a blank look) … He asked the question, "If there is no God, then who should a man follow?" He answered his own question by saying a man should follow his own conscience. And you know what…? He's right: he should follow his own conscience. However, it's in his interest if his conscience agrees with my conscience.

Jesus has blasphemed twice, against God and the Roman Empire.

What do you think we should do with him, Rabbi? Do you think he is dangerous?

Yes.

Actually, I found him rather pleasant. I asked myself if we shouldn't use him for something to our advantage.

I can think of no way that someone who denies the existence of God can be of benefit to the earth. He's like a wild animal that cannot be trained.

But he is one of the calmest men I have ever seen.

What is calm on the outside can be fire on the inside. He's like the simmering volcano I've heard about in Pompeii. Just waiting to explode and destroy.

Destroy what?

The Kingdom of God and the Roman Empire.

But he wants no followers. How can he destroy anything if he has no followers?

The rabbi took a few seconds to think about this question. He rarely thought before he spoke. His answers were automatic. His mind was a machine.

I will talk to him, Pontius Pilate. I will find out what is in the depth of his heart. If he denies God he should have the ultimate punishment.

Death?

Of course.

Does that mean I should be put to death because I don't believe in your god Jehovah? Should all Greeks and Romans be put to death because their gods are different from yours.

The rabbi did not know what to say.

Rabbi, our Roman gods are many, some are even rather fickle and act in odd ways sometimes.

But you have your top god, Jupiter.

Why do you have only one God, one King of the universe, one Almighty Creator? Maybe many gods were needed to create the world…

The rabbi hesitated again.

Of course I have the greatest respect for you, Pontius Pilate. You are a Roman and my ruler. But this man Jesus is a Jew.

What does that matter? His birth is not his fault.

He is a traitor to the kingdom of the Jews.

But maybe he is a friend to the Romans.

The rabbi's eyes pinched almost closed.

I will talk to him, Pontius Pilate. I will see what is in his heart.

You have my leave to do so, Rabbi. Come back when you have spoken with this interesting man, this Jesus of Nazareth.

XXXI

When Jesus was walking home from the olive grove, he met Paul.

Jesus, I have just been speaking with John. I think you are going too far. With your honesty you are putting yourself in danger.

But I hurt no man nor animal. I threaten nobody.

You hurt the hearts of the rabbis and you threaten the power of Pontius Pilate.

If one little man named Jesus can hurt the hearts of the rabbis, then the rabbis' hearts are very weak.

No man likes his god attacked.

Then his god is weak and he is weaker.

Jesus, Pontius Pilate called you to his palace. That is serious. You must be concerned.

Maybe he simply wanted to talk to me, like you, John, Matthew and Mark do. Maybe he's lonely in such a large palace and in need of a friend.

This is no time to joke. He fears you are stirring up the people.

I want no followers. I want no trouble. I have done nothing wrong.

What is right for you might be wrong for Pontius Pilate… and the rabbis…

That is why men want gods… to tell them what is right and wrong. But I fear the gods are mute. It is only men speaking about what is right and wrong, men pretending they know who the gods are and what they want. But I fear the gods are all human fabrications.

But Jesus, how can you say the gods do not exist?

How can you say they do? Can you say that all gods are true? Of course not. No one thinks the Roman gods, the Greek gods, and the Jewish god are all real… Paul, all I say is that when I look at the world, I see no proof for any god or gods. I must be honest with myself. Just because the rabbis say something is true doesn't mean it is. The same goes for the Romans and the Greeks and the philosophers and the sages. Life is a great mystery. I don't know from where life came, what governs life, what moves the sun and the stars, or anything else for that matter. The only thing I know is what moves my heart.

And what is that Jesus?

Mary… Mary and the mystery of all things.

Paul froze like a statue. His eyes were blank. He shuddered himself free and spoke.

You must be careful, Jesus. You must be careful about what you say and to whom you say it.

I will say what I think. I will not hide behind a veil of lies. My only goal is to light the way to the truth.

Maybe people don't want the truth. Maybe the dark glass of this world isn't enough for them. Maybe man needs a higher world, a world behind the veil of death, suffering, and pain.

Of this, there is no doubt. But if that higher world is not real, if this world is all there is, then there is only one solution… love.

But there has to be more. There must be another world.

Why? Because the rabbis say so? Maybe the only reality is power… power and love. And love is the opposite of power. Only in love does power lose its meaning. What if, in all of our relationships, everything is just a question of power...? One man trying to get something from another... one man trying to control another... But in love this disappears... In love two people have the same goal... their desires become one... their minds and bodies fuse... there is no struggle for power because there is no separation... That is why love is so rare, Paul... Because people never find another person with whom they can share the world... I have found Mary. She is my truth. She is my salvation.

Jesus looked at the blue sky and thought of Mary. His body tingled and pulsed. Paul thought of Mary, too. For Paul had no one to love.

XXXII

When Jesus and Mary lay on their straw bed before and after making love, there were often tears of joy, and most of them fell from Jesus's eyes. This was not because Jesus was more sensitive than Mary. No, not at all. It was simply because Mary's life had been more difficult and hence, it was far easier for Jesus to feel pure happiness. Mary had been through such hell on earth that moments of pure joy were very hard to come by. Joy was always tainted by memories of suffering. Jesus had suffered little. Mary had been an orphan. She had been used and abused. She'd had to scavenge for food and drink. As a child she had not been loved. Jesus, on the other hand, had known a mother and a father who'd fed him, clothed him, and loved him. When they died, they left him with a feeling that the world could be a warm place. So when he and Mary lay together on their bed talking, tears often found their way down his face.

I cannot imagine loving anyone else like I love you, Mary.

That is how I feel about you, Jesus.

I love everything about you, everything in you, all you are and have been.

And all of me loves all of you. I never imagined such love could be possible.

Nor did I Mary. When I look at you in these moments I cannot hold back the tears that dampen my cheeks.

I love it when you cry. You are my baby.

I am your baby, your brother, your husband, and your father. I am all men to you and you are all women to me. When I suck your breast I am your child. When I hold you I am your father. When we make love I am your husband.

And you are my god.

And you my goddess.

How can the world be so beautiful?

I don't know, but it is.

And Mary's fire was still burning. And Jesus's rod was ablaze anew. And the world was the kingdom of heaven.

XXXIII

Paul had known Mary as a harlot. Now he knew her as Jesus's lover. As he walked home, he was overcome with a jealousy that tore at every corner of his gut. He had had women, but he had never had love. His thoughts were angry and acerb:

Why does she love Jesus and not me?

How can she love a man who does not believe in God and who does not believe in another world, a world so much better than this one? This world is a hellhole, full of suffering and ugliness.

Jesus is a doubter. He is not God-fearing. What does she see in him? She must love his body. How could she love his mind?

Jesus only loves himself. He pretends that he loves other people. He pretends that he loves this world. But, no, he thinks he is God or the son of God. He thinks only of his own glory.

What is wrong with my body? Why don't women love me? Women have followed Jesus since hair started to grow on his face. He has had many women. He says he loves Mary. But that has to be a lie. I'm sure he only uses her for his pleasure. Why doesn't she love me?

What is it about Jesus that people like? His walk? His talk? His smile? Let him speak his doubts about God to the rabbis and the world. Let him tell Pontius Pilate his silly version of "truth." Let him get himself nailed to a cross… Then I'll have Mary. She is a beautiful woman. It is me she must love… No, I can't wait until Jesus is gone to have her. I will go see her tomorrow… tomorrow when she is selling her vegetables in the marketplace. I will get her to love me… She will forget about Jesus of Nazareth. She will love Paul… Paul of Palestine… One day I will establish a new religion. I will change the world… Mary and I will sit at God's side in heaven… together… forever.

Paul's plan was simple. He would first get Mary on his side. Then he would get Jesus killed. The martyr. Mankind loves martyrs. Then the most important part of his plan… he would have Mary and a few other women pretend they saw Jesus come back to life after he was dead. They would say Jesus had been resurrected. Paul would then tell the world that Jesus had died for the sins of mankind and he would promise that all weak and suffering people would get to the Kingdom of Heaven if they repented of their sins and followed him. It was a beautiful plan. The world is full of weak and suffering people. All he had to do was convince people that Jesus really was the Son of God and that His resurrection (witnessed by Mary and others) was proof. He could even say that Jesus's mother had been more than human, special, a virgin, and that God had implanted His seed in her. Then he – Paul – would marry Mary. She would love him and the world would love him because he, Paul of Palestine, had the solution for saving the world. He would, single-handedly, take the world out of its misery. He would promise a better world. And mankind would follow him because mankind was weak and paltry.

Paul's plan was lucid. He would start working on it the following morning.

XXXIV

Mary and Jesus made love five times that night. They loved each other to life and death. Theirs was not a love of calculation. There was no "I do this for you and you do that for me." Every gesture was full of tenderness and desire. Every word they spoke to each other was truth. They were locked together like no two people had ever been locked together before. When morning came and they looked into each other's eyes, it was as if they were looking in the mirror… Mary was Jesus, Jesus was Mary, man was woman, woman was man. Man and woman had fused. And yes, one of Jesus's sperms had made its way up the river of Mary's fertile belly. A sperm and an egg had united. Creation. A baby. A child. Life… Dogs do it. Donkeys do it. Birds do it. Even trees and plants have a way of doing it. Life: it goes on and on. It is everywhere.

What is not everywhere is love. Love: Mary and Jesus. It is so rare and it can't go on and on. Why not? Death. It too is everywhere.

Paul let the sun rise above the treetops before going to find Mary in the marketplace. He had hardly slept that night, with his plan firing through his head. Never before had he felt such excitement.

Good morning, my dear Mary.

Morning Paul.

How's business? Your vegetables always look the finest in the market.

I'm not sure about that.

You're also the most beautiful of the vegetable sellers.

There is only one man who truly appreciates my beauty.

No Mary, you are mistaken on two counts… I too appreciate your beauty and Jesus is only using you for his own satisfaction.

How can you say such a thing, Paul? You know nothing about the love Jesus and I have for each other.

But I do know what kind of a man Jesus is. He doubts the existence of God. He does not believe in truth. He fears no other man, not even Pontius Pilate or the rabbis.

That is partly why I love him. He's a man, not a mouse.

But Mary, such a man is only trouble. He will soon be put to death. Your love will be in vain. Don't you see? You should love me, not Jesus. A man who does not love God, cannot truly love a woman.

How can you say such things about your friend? You, Paul, are not a friend, you're a traitor. You don't know Jesus like I know him.

When he's dead, we'll talk again.

Stop suggesting he'll die.

He must stop suggesting there's no God.

He doesn't say there's no God. He says he has seen no proof of a god. He says the Romans have their gods, the Greeks have their gods, and the Jews have their One Almighty God. He says some of these gods must be false. It is possible they all are.

But Mary, a man like Jesus goes against the grain.

He walks alone. He will die alone.

No. When he dies, my heart will die with him. We are one. We are a single body of love.

Paul could see that he was getting nowhere with Mary. She would have to wait. He would go find the rabbi who sat on Pontius Pilate's council.

Well Mary, I must be going. The days are getting shorter. Winter is coming.

Goodbye Paul.

Goodbye Mary, and think on my words.

I already have.

The man who would found the Christian Church walked off moving left and right as he made his way through the crowds.

XXXVI

The rabbi didn't need to be convinced that Jesus was a dangerous man; he had thought it for years.

Paul, my friend, any man who doubts the existence of God is a threat not only to Palestine, but to the world.

Yes.

And what I fear the most is that Jesus is sure that he himself is God.

It's not clear, Rabbi. Sometimes he says he is God and sometimes he says he is the Messiah that the Jews have been waiting for. I think he has hallucinations. In any case I heard him in the marketplace yesterday saying that if there was no life after death – if there was no God – then we must worship this life... He started stirring the people with his charisma. He told them that they should be slaves to nobody – neither rabbi nor Roman!

His charisma makes him all the more dangerous. I'll tell Pilate immediately. We, as Jews, must protect our kingdom, and Pontius Pilate, as the ruler of Palestine, must protect the safety of our land.

At least Paul's day had not been wasted. The rabbi would inform Pilate that things were getting worse, that Jesus was trying to incite the masses. This, of course, was a total lie. Jesus never preached his ideas; he revealed them only to a few close friends. The one thing that was partially true was that Jesus believed that if there was no life after death, then this world took on ultimate value… to waste this life would become the greatest sin of all. But Jesus also knew that men were perhaps no freer than animals or the moon and sun. They were what they were and they could not be otherwise. The world could not be saved. It would always be what it was: a great machine that man was simply a part of that turned and turned and could never be stopped. Man would always have false gods and false prophets and strange values. That was man and he would never crawl out of his hole and into the light of a so-called "truth." Man was like a blind bat flying frantically in the night trying to find a home that didn't exist. Mankind was as innocent as any infant ever born.

Paul would never have Mary. He would find other women to help him carry out his plan; weak women to whom love was as foreign as it was to him.

XXXVII

Darling Jesus, I have been looking everywhere for you.

I was walking in the olive grove and thinking about our love. The world has taken on a different glow since I met you. I used to see much more ugliness; now I see much more beauty.

What one sees is always a function of what is inside the body that has the gazing eyes. Our love has changed the colours and textures of the world. I love you. I love the world.

I love us. I love our world.

But there is a part of our world that I do not love today, Jesus. Your friend Paul came to me in the marketplace this morning. He tried to tell me that I was wasting my love on you. He wanted to pull me from you. He said you were a dangerous man and that you would surely die soon.

Such behaviour doesn't surprise me at all. Paul is a sad man, a weak man. He does not have the strength to understand or appreciate our love. I don't think he knows what it is to love another person. I find that sad.

He is a dangerous man. He wants to destroy the most beautiful thing on Earth; our love.

I don't know if he ever will feel real love. It's not something one can teach to another. It must grow and blossom within one's own heart.

I told Paul that he knew nothing about the feelings we have for each other.

And you're right. A love like ours is one of the rarest things on this earth. There is only one sun; perhaps there is only one Mary-and-Jesus.

And it's sad because love is what can make the world a better place.

Yes. People who love respect the rest of the world. Look at us. We wake up every morning so grateful to be alive. We can't wait to see the sun and have another day together on Earth. We love life. People like Paul don't love this world at all. They dream of another world. That is why they create all their gods: to save them from "this life." This is my only real message to the world: the kingdom of God is not in the next life, it is here… now. This life is the only life we can be sure of. All the gods and afterlives might be pure chimera, creations of sick minds and sick people.

Yes, Jesus. God must be inside each human, each creature, each existing thing.

You are wise, wonderful, and beautiful, Mary. I love you to death. And where there is love, there is life. God is love. God is life.

Mary and Jesus fell into each other's arms and onto the straw bed. They could do nothing else. When they finished making love, it was usually Jesus who spoke first. This time it was Mary.

Jesus, darling, your friend Paul is convinced that you are in danger because of your ideas.

Paul's my friend because I am friends with all men. He is the reason I am in danger. He spreads falsehoods about my ideas. He neither understands me nor my vision of the world.

Neither do most men.

The longer I live, the more I think that's true. Most people's eyes cannot see very far. It's not their fault. They are weak and so are their eyes. Lately I have been thinking about how people always want to see a cause and a creator behind everything. They want a reason for everything. The world must have a reason! Life must have a reason! Everything that happens must have a reason. When lightning strikes the earth, people want to say, "Ah, it is an act of God… God is angry with us because of something we have done." But it is very possible that God has absolutely nothing to do with the lightning. The lightning might simply be caused by an infinity of things in nature. When there is a flood, the rabbis say that God is punishing man for his sins. But maybe the flood has nothing to do with God and sin. People want simple answers for everything. That is the way the human mind works. It wants simple causes, simple connections, simple dichotomies like good and evil. And Mary, it is very possible that man sees the world in a way that is completely false.

I have thought the same…

Perhaps God is not the cause of anything. Perhaps there was no creation like the Bible says. Perhaps there is no good and evil like the Bible says. Perhaps the whole universe is a big machine that has been turning forever and will continue to turn forever. Perhaps man is just a tiny cog in the great wheel of existence. Perhaps thunder just happens like everything else just happens. Of course, one can find reasons, but what are the reasons behind those reasons? And the reasons behind those reasons? Perhaps everything is infinitely and eternally linked together. Perhaps all causes are built into the nature of the world.

But Jesus, men can't think this way. They must have their gods. When things go wrong, they must have their evil and their guilty.

And because they don't love this life, they must have their world-after-this-world. Yes. Men can't imagine that this world might simply exist without a cause or a reason. They cannot imagine that the earth, moon and stars have no beginning and no end and no higher reason for existing. But it is very possible that there is no ultimate cause for anything. Everything might just be. Man, monkey, moon, water, wheat, wine, weather, grass, stars, kings, slaves, fish and insects all linked together... all nature... all together... alone... because there is nothing else that can be...

Most people cannot fathom such thoughts.

So I ask myself if I am dangerous... and if I am in danger...

You are not dangerous, Jesus. You love life. Life is a miracle for you. You respect the biggest and the smallest creatures. But you must be careful about Paul. He is trying to create trouble for you. Of that I'm sure.

Paul is like thunder and lightning or a coiled and poisonous snake. His actions could be nefarious, but… so are many other things in the world.

You must be vigilant, my love.

I will. But if the authorities come back and ask questions, I will tell them the truth.

But the truth is dangerous.

That is why I keep it to myself most of the time. But Mary, the real the truth is that I don't even pretend to know the truth. What I think I do know is that the way most men see the world is probably very un-true. It's the lies of the world that are dangerous. The lies of the world that act like fences for sheep. To keep the sheep inside. The lies keep the masses under control… But then again, maybe the fences are necessary? Maybe truth really is the most dangerous thing for mankind. Maybe Paul and the rabbis are right… maybe I am dangerous…

I'm worried Jesus. I'm worried they'll take you from me.

To separate us would be the greatest tragedy I can imagine.

Yes.

The only thing that can break our love is death.
And that's why we treasure our lives.
I love you Mary Magdalene.
I love you Jesus of Nazareth.

XXXVIII

The next morning Jesus decided to go to the marketplace to find Paul. As he was walking through the crowd, an old woman fell to the ground in front of him, dropping her basket. She lay motionless.

She's dead! someone shouted.

She has been stricken by the devil! another called.

A crowd gathered around the old woman and stared. Jesus knelt down beside her and took her right hand. He gently rubbed the palm and the fingers. Then he bent forward and ran his fingers through her grizzled, matted grey hair.

Bless you, he said softly. *May life continue to breathe inside you.*

A few seconds later the woman opened her eyes.

She saw Jesus and said, *Where am I?*

You are in Nazareth. You are still on this beautiful earth, Jesus answered.

The woman's lips slowly separated and a delicate smile appeared.

He has saved her, a man shouted. *Jesus has performed another miracle! He has saved this old woman from the arms of death!* It was the voice of Paul who had pushed his way through the crowd.

Jesus said nothing. He and another man helped the woman to her feet. A young girl gathered the things that had fallen from her basket.

Are you okay? Jesus asked.

I think so. I don't know what happened. I suddenly felt like I had no blood in my head.

Hopefully you'll be fine. Can you walk alone?

I will walk with her, the little girl said.

And what's your name? Jesus asked.

Romée.

What a lovely name. Are you from Rome?

Where is that? the girl asked. She was half Jesus's size, probably six or seven years old.

Rome is where the Emperor lives. It is far away in the direction of where the sun comes every morning. Many soldiers come from there. Is your father a soldier?

I am a child of the world. My mother says the world is my father.

Your mother is wise. We are all children of this world. We are all children of God. It is good of you to walk with this woman to be sure she is all right.

The old woman looked at Jesus, then took the little girl's hand.

Jesus of Nazareth, you truly are a man of God, she said.

Many in the crowd had listened to this conversation. Now everyone began to disperse. People chattered about the miracle they had witnessed. Paul came and stood close to Jesus.

Why call it a miracle, Paul? You know it wasn't. I didn't bring her back to life. She never died.

People need miracles, Paul said.

I came to the market looking for you. We must talk.

And they talked. But talking did nothing to change Paul's vision of the world or how he saw himself and Jesus therein.

XXXIX

The smell. The mind. The past. The touch. The skin. The blemishes. The feet. The way he or she makes love. The nose, eyes, fingers, arms, legs, hair, belly, mouth, shape, nape, when asleep and awake. The sound of the voice. What the voice utters. The walk, talk, and smile. Have you ever known another person about whom you loved everything? Absolutely everything.

This was the case with Jesus and Mary. The world was about to destroy this love. The world did not know that such a love was possible. Not Pontius Pilate. Not the rabbis. Certainly not Paul, John, Luke, or Matthew or any other of Jesus's friends. No one understood how Mary and Jesus felt about each other. There might be other such couples later on as the world spun its lonely path through space. Romeo and Juliet. Tristan and Isolde. Elizabeth Taylor and Richard Burton. John and Yoko… Who knows? But up until 0 AD there had never been a love like the love Jesus and Mary had for each other.

When Jesus was sentenced to die on the cross with a few other local petty thieves, the absurdity and stupidity of the world was at what one might call "an ordinary zenith." Paul continued to spread rumours that Jesus was the Messiah and a performer of miracles. The rabbi who advised Pontius Pilate thought Jesus was a threat to the stability of Palestine and was loosening the rabbinical hold on the hearts and minds of the people. Pontius Pilate, though even a bit fond of Jesus, didn't really care much either way and, for him, sending a man to his death was not much different than taking a pee. Life was not worth much. And it still isn't. Today some people give value to certain aspects of life: community, large mammals, money, cars, gods, sports teams, large houses, jewellery… But few people, if any, give value to all that exists. The whole universe never gets the same status as the local shit. Small animals never get the status of large ones. Animals are never up with people. Trees, flowers, and all that grows from the ground never get the status of creatures with blood. Rocks and dirt always lag behind so-called "living" things. This has always made people like Jesus chuckle because rocks and moons and planets have been around for millions and billions of years, but they're not considered alive.

Sure, there have been pockets of people who respected more than the average Joe… some tribes of American Indians, Buddhists, and maybe a few others. But all in all the people of the world have never been very nice to the whole of existence. And their glorious gods have always tended to exacerbate the problem.

So, to put it simply, there was only one Christian and he died on the cross. What came after him had little or nothing to do with his vision of the world. What came to be called Christianity was not about Jesus Christ. It was the work of a weak sad man named Paul. It should have been called Paulianity. Paul did not love life or the world. And the world did not love him. He used Jesus to create a world wherein he had a place, wherein he became important. But this was not Jesus's world. In Jesus's world there was no concept of sin or the devil.

Nobody was sacrificed for the sins of the world. There was no Heaven or Hell or Judgment Day. There was no virgin mother. There was no resurrection of the dead, no hate of the body, no belief in an eternal soul. All these things came from the unhappy mind of a man who did not love this world.

When Pontius Pilate called Jesus back to his palace a second time, the eggs were already fried. The rabbi had convinced the governor of Palestine that Jesus was a nuisance. He was getting people to think for themselves. This has always been a danger for those in power.

Jesus did not believe in things unseen. But neither did he believe that the human mind was, necessarily, capable of grasping the truth. And maybe the truth was like a serpent that could bite itself in the butt.

Jesus simply respected life. All life. Being. The whole bag of marbles. He didn't pick and choose what was of value. Everything was of value. He didn't claim to know where the world came from. He didn't claim to know what was behind the world. He didn't claim to know what caused what. He had no idea if the mind was free or if the whole idea of *free will* was a human invention that had absolutely nothing to do with reality. It was all a great great mystery to him.

In the end, Jesus knew two things:

Life is rampant and death is rampant. Both beauty and tragedy are everywhere. In such a world it is hard for a thinking man not to go crazy.

If there's a god, its name should be Love. His love for Mary was his salvation.

Jesus carried the cross to the top of the hill. As soon as he set it down, the Roman soldiers told him to lie on his back on top of it. He stared at the empty blue sky as the soldiers tied his body to the wood. Then they drove spikes through his wrists and ankles. It took four soldiers to lift the cross and plant it in a hole in the ground. The petty thieves got the same treatment.

This barbarism is the image that Paul used to define his religion. He could have used the image of Jesus and Mary in each other's arms the night before in the throes of ecstasy as they made love for the last time. Had Jesus made a religion, this is probably what he would have done.

Jesus said a few things on the cross... *Forgive them for they know not what they do... The kingdom of God is here and now within you…* that kind of thing. But, of course, all that got lost in the shuffle of history as Christianity expanded with Islam, Buddhism, and Hinduism and locked its arms around a good part of the world.

Night was coming. The moment Jesus expired, Mary was the only person at the foot of the cross. Paul and the others had left hours before when their friend had stopped talking. Mary lay on her back and stared at the same sky Jesus had looked at that morning as he was being attached to the two wooden planks. As the heavens darkened a few scattered stars were beginning to twinkle. Mary had brought the tattered blanket under which she and Jesus had slept during the last three years of his life on the earth. She curled her body inside it placing both hands on her slightly inflated belly. Before she was asleep, one hand crawled out to wipe away the few final drops of blood that fell on the face that the dead man on the cross had so adored.

VOL. 11

MARY & GOD

Night was coming. The moment Jesus expired, Mary was the only person at the foot of the cross. Paul and the others had left hours before when their friend had stopped talking. Mary lay on her back and stared at the same sky Jesus had looked at that morning as he was being attached to the two wooden planks. As the heavens darkened a few scattered stars were beginning to twinkle. Mary had brought the tattered blanket that she and Jesus had slept under for the last three years. She curled her body inside it placing both hands on her slightly inflated belly. Before she was asleep, one hand crawled out to wipe away the few final drops of blood that fell on the face that the dead man on the cross had so adored.

XL

Two months before Jesus's barbaric crucifixion, he and Mary Magdalene had made love like no two people had done before. Why? Simply because no two humans had ever loved each other as much as Jesus and Mary loved. They were the real Adam and Eve. Each adored every aspect of the other's being. Each respected every moment of the other's life. Each constantly felt the miracle of being alive. It was easier for Jesus to love than Mary, because he had been given love as a boy. He knew what love was when he was a child. Mary didn't. She'd had none growing up. She had been an orphan and had had to fend for herself. She was actually stronger than Jesus. She had to invent love. She had to turn Hell into Heaven. She had to rise above the coldness of the world and learn to love. Jesus just took the love he had received as a child, expanded it, and spread it around. Mary had to rewrite the script of her life. That happened when she met Jesus. Love became a real possibility. Love was no longer a foreign country. The most important thing was that little by little she began to realise that Jesus really did love her. She slowly but surely began to love herself. The more she loved herself, the more she loved Jesus. And the more she loved Jesus, the more Jesus loved her. The more Jesus loved her, the more she loved Jesus. They fused. When they made love there was no separation. Eventually they were always making love, even when apart.

So two months before Jesus was nailed to the cross, Mary became pregnant. Seven months after his absurd death she gave birth to a boy. They had decided to name him "God" – God Magdalene Christ. He was born in the home Jesus's father had built, the same home where Jesus and Mary had lived for three wonderful years before his murder, for murder it was by the powers that were in place more than two thousand years ago in the area around Jerusalem.

Though fatherless, God had a wonderful

childhood. Mary loved him like she had loved Jesus. And Mary taught him to love the world in return. She taught him to appreciate everything, especially being alive. She instilled in God a feeling for the mystery of life, all life. As a child God would look at his hands and wonder where the five fingers came from — and why five and not three or twelve? He would breathe and feel the air rush in and out of his nose and throat, and when he would exhale he would put his hand in front of his mouth and the air would tickle his skin. Sometimes when Mary would talk to him he would put a finger in each ear and her voice would disappear. How did these ears work? How did sounds form in his mother's mouth and travel into his ears? And when he would put bread into his mouth, he would realise that his mouth and teeth would chew without thinking, as if his body knew on its own that it had to grind up the food so it could pass into his body. How could a body know what to do without a head giving it instructions? Where did thoughts and feelings come from? When he would run through the hills, he wondered how his legs worked, what propelled them? Why could birds and butterflies fly, but not him and his mother Mary?

What fascinated God most were his eyes. He would close them and there was nothing except some funny patterns that seemed to sparkle a bit in the dark. But then when he would open them again there was the world he was used to. What an amazing circus of lines and colours and movement! Often he would go to the marketplace with his mother and sit for hours and watch the lines and colours dance in front of him. What a kaleidoscope! He wondered if other eyes saw the same lines and colours that he was seeing. He wondered if animal eyes saw differently than people eyes. And he asked himself if what he was seeing was "real", whether maybe his eyes were "wrong" and other eyes were "right", or whether maybe there was no such thing as right and wrong when it came to seeing.

When God reached age twelve he had a strange feeling that his eyes always saw only the surface of things and in seeing the surface, they never got to the "reality" of anything. He wondered if and how anybody could get to the reality… *maybe there was no reality…*

Yes, God was a curious boy and Mary fed his curiosity. She would listen and smile and tell him how his mind so resembled that of his father. He would tell her about insects he had followed and examined — ants, beetles, and spiders. *Where do they come from? How long have they been on earth? Are they happy? Do they feel pain, joy, love, hunger, fear? Do they ever get lonely? What makes them move forward? What tells them to stop? How do they get all those legs to work in unison? Are they obeying orders?* Then God would ask his mother the same questions about people. *Why do people do what* they *do? How do their bodies work? What makes an arm or a tongue or a foot move...?*

God had many friends as he was nice to people. He was happy; he made others happy in turn. He would smile infinitely more than he would frown. He laughed much more than he cried. Many things made him laugh, but only two things made him cry, and one of those things was joy. Sometimes he would walk through the world and be so happy that tears of joy would roll from the corners of his eyes. The other thing that made him cry was death, the death of people or animals large and small. He hated death. His mother would tell him that he had to accept it, that it was part of "life", but he still hated the thought of creatures he loved disappearing forever. "But it might not be forever,"

Mary would say. "But, mother," God would answer, "what if it *is?*"

He was, however, saddened by the fact that, except for his mother, the other people in Judea didn't care about his ideas and questions. They didn't wonder about why things were the way they were. They didn't marvel at the moon and stars, the sea, the sky, the earth and all creatures thereon. They always acted like everything was normal and there was no reason to ask questions about anything. When he would ask someone where everything came from or why things were this or that way, the person would just quote the Bible and say Jehovah made it all in six days. *How,* wondered God, *could people be satisfied with such simplistic answers? How could people live with their heads in the sand?* But they did and, little by little, he realised that that's just the way people were. Little by little he learned not to expect too much from his friends and acquaintances. But also, little by little, God began to feel more and more alone. The noise of the marketplace began to tire him. His friends started to bore him and he in turn bored them. There was only one friend with whom he could really talk: Joshua, who was thought to be the son of Marcus, the Roman soldier, yet there was no certainty about this given that Joshua's mother, Deborah, was said to be a harlot. "That poor boy will never know who his real father is," the Jews would say. "When your mother is a whore, Satan is always your father."

When hair commenced to grow above and below God's lips, his thoughts about his father multiplied. *Who really was this man people were sometimes calling the "Son of Jehovah"? How could he possibly have died for the sins of the world as certain people were murmuring? How could he have been resurrected when nothing else was "resurrected"? Why Jesus? There were plenty of other good people who were nailed to crosses by the Romans…*

God did not believe what he was hearing about his father. Mary had told him that Jesus had not believed in the concept of "sin" or in the veracity of the Jewish God. So God did not believe that Jesus was the son of Jehovah any more than he thought his friend Joshua was the son of the devil.

L

It was the man Paul that started spreading the word about Jesus being divine. God watched Paul wander through the streets trying to get people to listen to him. Mary had told her son that Paul was a sad man, a sick man, a man who did not love the world the way Jesus had. She said the truth was that Paul hated the world. "Isn't this why he is trying to start a new religion, a religion based on another world, an afterlife, a better world, a kingdom of God in Heaven?" she said one evening when they were having supper. God knew his father never thought any of this. His father had been sure of only one thing: life on this earth, the here and now, what he could see, touch, and feel. Jesus had loved the world for what it was. He had accepted it. Of course he had wanted to try to make it better, but not by telling lies about another world. Jesus Christ had done what he could, but he had never preached a "Supreme Being" that had created man and the earth and who promised another life in some mysterious kingdom, where hell, fire, and damnation would be the lot of the so-called "sinners", and milk, honey, and eternal happiness would be waiting for all the good boys and girls! No, God knew that his father had never said such things. His father had never made promises he couldn't keep. His father had been a lover of the earth he walked on, not of some ethereal land of angels and devils… Jesus had talked about loving this life. Jesus had marvelled at this life. The blood of the miracle of existence had constantly flowed through his veins. But after his death, God watched Paul turn all this inside out. He watched Paul take all the mystery out of life and start a religion based on suffering, fear, and his hate of his own flesh. He watched Paul use the horrendous image of his father agonising on the cross as the symbol of the new church. He watched Paul spread the news that Jesus, Son of Jehovah, had been resurrected and had gone to Heaven. Then he heard Paul tell the people that if they too wanted to go to Heaven, they had to listen to him, Paul, the great Truth Sayer, and do what he said. It was a grand formula… a magic formula… And then, to top it all off, Paul came up with the Virgin Mary, a woman having a child without needing a man. Why? Because he, Paul, had never known the pleasures of the body. He had never had a woman who loved him. He had been jealous of Jesus who shared the deepest love with God's mother, Mary Magdalene. Paul had to create a virgin mother, a virgin birth. Paul made virginity pure. Jesus had made love pure. His love for Mary had been the purest thing on earth.

So what happened? How did the world unfold? God's father, Jesus Christ, unwittingly became the object of a million lies and a million promises, none of which would be kept. Jesus was not the son of God; God was the son of Jesus. The so-called "Christian" religion that Paul and his friends invented has nothing to do with Jesus. It has nothing to do with God. The Old Testament and the New Testament are only testaments of the people who wrote them; people who saw the world as a wicked, evil, dirty, sinful place where the weak and the unhappy yearn for another life, another world… Can they be blamed for this? Of course not. When one is suffering one seeks a release from one's pain. This was Paul. This was the origin of Christianity.

LI

When God and Joshua were sixteen, they often walked and talked in the olive grove where Mary and Jesus had strolled the first day they met. One day their conversation went like this:

My parents used to come here often.
How do you know that?
My mother has told me so.
You're lucky. You know who your father is.
No, I don't. I never knew my father. I know his name and I've heard stories about him. But, I never saw him, never touched him, never talked to him… If Marcus is your father, then you are luckier than I am.
What do you mean?
You will have seen him alive. You will have been

able to watch him move and hear his voice. Me, I never saw Jesus do anything.

And if Marcus is not my father?

Then you are in a situation similar to mine… You may never see the man that made you… Joshua, every situation can be turned inside out. You can always find a good side and a bad side to anything. And everybody does it in his or her own way. Look at the man Paul. He has taken my father's murder and is turning it into a religion. The world is a crazy place. It can go in so many crazy directions… Look at love. The more you love someone, the more pain you will feel when you lose the love. Even the "possibility" of losing love is painful. If you don't love, you'll never have to endure the pain of its loss…

How do you know this? Have you loved?

No, but my mother has told me. We talk about such things all the time.

You are lucky to have a mother like you have.

And I am lucky to have a friend like you. You and my mother are really the only people I can talk to.

I have a mother, but we don't talk that much.

All mothers are different.

All fathers are different. Some are so different they are invisible.

Like mine…

I just wish people would stop calling me a "bastard". No one likes to be called such a thing.

And no one should be called a "bastard". It's not your fault if you don't know who your father is. People are weak. People are dumb. They only belittle others to try to enlarge themselves. But it never works.

Ah, God is talking… I like to hear God speak.

Joshua, we are surrounded by simple people. They follow their Bible. They are like sheep following a shepherd. You cannot blame them.

I don't blame them. But I wish they would stop looking down on my mother and me. In the marketplace I once heard that crazy man Paul say that your father preached that no man has the right to judge another man.

That is one of the few truths Paul teaches. My mother has told me many times that my father never judged or condemned people. The problem with Paul is that he says that my father also said that the Almighty Jehovah can and will judge people… everybody! He will send some to "Hell" and others to "Heaven." My mother assures me that my father did not believe in the reality of an Almighty Jehovah, nor did he ever talk about Heaven and Hell, except how life here on Earth can be both very beautiful and very ugly.

But God, Paul insists that your father was the son of Jehovah.

You being the son of Marcus is much more likely than my father being the son of Jehovah. My father's father was named Joseph and his mother was called Mary like my mother.

Why does Paul say that your father's mother was a virgin?

He is trying to glorify my father and set him apart. Religions need "miracles" and new twists to things. Paul "twists" almost everything that ever came out of my father's mouth.

Why would your father's mother… your grandmother Mary… why would her being a virgin help to glorify your father?

That is a great question, Joshua. Paul is strange. He seems to be a very unhappy man.

What does your mother say about what Paul is doing?

She laughs. She says he is a weak deluded creature and that everything he is doing grows out of his unhappy pitiful life. Do you know that he tried to seduce my mother once?

How do you know?

She told me. She said he once came to her in the marketplace and told her that loving Jesus was stupid and a lost cause. He said that Jesus was going to die soon and that she should love him, Paul!

And after Jesus died…? Did he try again?

Many men have tried. But she has loved none of them.

She is a beautiful woman.

So is your mother, Joshua. All mothers are beautiful. Without them, nothing would exist.

Then all fathers are beautiful too. Without them, nothing would exist.

Then consider your father a beautiful man… even if you don't know who he is.

I will try.

It does no good to be unhappy about things you cannot control.

You are wise, God, as wise as a butterfly.

I doubt it. I too can be unhappy. Butterflies are never unhappy.

How do you know that?

I don't…

And it came to pass that God and Joshua continued

their stroll back down the hill toward the marketplace where the herds were going about their business, where Joshua was called a bastard, and where God Magdalene Christ and his mother were both seen to be floating down a different river.

LII

While God was working on a pair of shoes, he
started thinking about names and words: *God
Magdalene Christ is as good a name as any. What is
in a name anyway? How do words go from foreign
sounds to common sounds? At first all words sound
strange. But if you hear them enough, and say them
enough, they become perfectly ordinary. Even big
words like "teleology" or "hieroglyphic" can sound
ordinary. Who invented the first words? Why are there
different languages? Greek... Latin... Aramaic... I
wonder about the word "Jehovah." The Bible says that
Jehovah did this and Jehovah did that. Why isn't
Jehovah named "Butterfly"? At least butterflies exist
and can be seen and touched. Aren't butterflies as
divine as Jehovah? The word "butterfly" is more*

beautiful than "Jehovah", especially in Latin. My mother taught me the word when I was eight years old. My father had taught her... "papillo" or "papillionus"... But what makes a word beautiful or ugly anyway? (God knew that Jehovah was also called "God", but that depended on which language one was speaking. In Latin it was "Deus", which one day might sound like a score in a tennis game...) *Why are people who speak a language well or in a certain way considered more intelligent than people who don't speak that way. What do words have to do with intelligence? Butterflies don't talk and they do all kinds of intelligent things. Perhaps my mother and I don't speak the way so-called "intelligent" people speak, but...*

God's mind wandered, but his shoes were well made and popular. Even the Roman soldiers bought them. Joshua's might-be father, Marcus, was the first one to buy a pair of God's shoes and he told his friends about them. Of course they were really more like sandals than shoes, but what difference did that make? They were comfortable and kept rocks and splinters from cutting one's feet.

LIII

The days and nights of God's life had become many. Thousands and thousands had passed. The sun – O what a mystery it was! It came and went. But what was it? How big was it? How far away was it? What was it made of? Why did it change size and colour? Why was it orange or red? Why was it never cut in half high in the sky like the moon? Was it the sun that made the days warm or cold? What caused the temperature of the world to change? Did the sun warm it and the moon cool it? But sometimes the days were cool and the nights were warm... God and Mary talked as they ate their bread and drank their wine at the table Jesus had made. She was now well over thirty, but still as beautiful as ever. God was tall and strong and beautiful like Jesus had been. Mary's memories of her great love were as solid and poignant as ever. She had never met another man like Jesus. A hole had been carved in her heart where Jesus lived every day, warm and safe like a mouse in a hole in the ground. One might imagine that she would have fallen in love with God. He moved like his father, had lips that cast the same silhouette, and even gave off the same odour. But Mary couldn't fall in love with God, because she was in love with him from the moment he existed, even when he was but a fetus in her womb. Jesus had made that baby with her. How could she not love it? But of course God-the-fetus, God-the-baby, God-the-child, and God-the-full-grown-sixteen-year-old were all different Gods. Mary often thought about how she had had to learn to love herself, and how in this world self-love is such a daunting task. How much more human time and effort is spent making people feel bad about themselves than good! How much more criticism and negative comparison there is compared to compliments and positive comparison! *The Jews and Paul only drive the nails of self-dislike deeper into defenseless human hearts! We are sinful! Our bodies are sinful! Our hearts are impure! We are evil and corrupt!*

Only the soul is pure! What soul? The one that will float to heaven when the trials and tribulations of this life are finally over! Yes Mary Magdalene, you had to learn to love yourself, but you did not have to learn to love God. Your love for him was built into the fabric of the universe. You had made God when you and Jesus were at the zenith of love in this world. Jesus knew how to love. He knew love was the only remedy for the unknown, for the mystery, for the chaos, for the pain and suffering on this earth… and for death! Wasn't death the greatest mystery of all? *No!* cried Jesus. *Love is the greatest mystery of all. For only love can conquer death!* That was the real message of Jesus: Love first; die later…!

Mary's mind often flew back to Jesus when she and God talked.

You know God, Mary said, *your father even loved animals and plants. He often said, "They are part of life, too. Why should they be of less value than anything else?"*

Not many people think like that.

No, they don't. The Jews say Jehovah created plants and animals so man could eat. Jesus would laugh at that idea and say, "Maybe Jehovah intended it to be the other way around — that animals should feed on men!"

Who knows?

Just know that your father respected it all. He could do no harm to any of it.

(So what happened? What did Christianity do after the only real Christian died on the cross? It killed millions of human beings because they were "evil." It ran swords and lances through the bodies of infidels and thought it was doing good. It went across the ocean and destroyed the Aztecs, Mayas, and Incas because they didn't believe in Jesus Christ. But Jesus Christ would never have killed a living creature, unless perhaps that creature was trying to kill him and other innocent peace-loving people. But he surely would never have killed one single solitary Inca, Aztec, Maya, and other American "Indian" because that person didn't believe in Him. He didn't believe in Him, not the man that Paul claimed was the son of Jehovah who had been crucified on the cross to save men from their sins so they could all meet in Heaven. No, he didn't believe in any of that. He believed in this life. He knew nothing of another life. He was too honest for that... God eventually lived over 2,000 years.

He travelled around the world and saw with his own eyes what the "Christians" did to each other and to non-Christians. Eventually he killed himself.)

LIV

Mary still kept a garden behind the small one-room house. Poor people stole from it sometimes, but she considered that she was giving rather than that they were taking. There were figs and dates, beans and cucumbers, and a small patch of coriander. From the day God was able to walk, Mary would take him to the garden with her so he would learn to appreciate what comes from the earth. After some years, one conversation went thus:

Mother, where do you think this all comes from?
I don't know God, but I love it. Is there anything better than a fresh fig?
Do you think figs – any plants – exist for "a reason"?
What do you mean?

The Jews say Jehovah put plants and animals on the earth for us... Do you think everything exists for "us"?

I have absolutely no idea God. No one knows. People always talk about "reasons" for things existing... and the "reasons" are usually related to themselves. People love to put themselves at the centre of the universe. But it is very possible that nothing – absolutely nothing – exists "for a reason". It might be that all existence "just exists" and people are part of it, like plants, animals, rocks, rivers, clouds, rain, and the sun.

Do you mean that we are no more important than a fig or a cucumber?

I didn't say that. This is something your father and I often talked about. Just because there is no "guiding hand" behind life doesn't mean that life is not important. Every creature must decide for itself what is important.

When you think of the world that way everything changes...

Of course it does. The rabbis no longer tell you what is important. Nor do the Romans or anyone else. You, God, must decide for yourself, and I, Mary, must decide for myself. This is one of the "reasons" why your father saw the world so differently from other people.

He didn't put man and Jehovah on top of the hierarchy of life. He saw no hierarchy. He saw a great struggle for power. The Jews with their Jehovah, the Romans with their deities and laws and armies, animals eating plants, men eating animals, the Romans conquering the Jews, and on and on. Your father used to say that if cucumbers had teeth, they would eat animals and maybe even us. None of this means that one thing is necessarily better or worse than another. The question is really what controls what.

So Mother, where should I look to know what is good or bad, right or wrong?

There is only one place to look and that is into your own heart.

How will I know how I should live?

Will you "know" or "feel"…? Your head and your heart will talk to each other, play with each other, and even sometimes fight with each other.

And who will win – my head or my heart?

That is for you to discover my dear God. But actually in the end they might be inextricably linked together. They might always decide everything together. That is part of the great mystery.

But Mother, everyone talks about there being good and evil in the world. Don't laws and commandments tell us the difference?

Dear God, all laws and commandments are made by people. The Romans have their version of good and bad. Pontius Pilate has his good and bad. The Jews have their good and bad. The man who beats his donkey thinks he is doing good, but maybe he is doing bad. Of course most people justify their good and bad with deities, a Jehovah, and so-called prophets. Your father believed in none of them. He was his own god, his own prophet. But he used to say that most people's ideas of good and bad were built into their systems like the blood that flows through their veins. He did not think most people were strong enough to create their own vision of good and evil.

I wish Father were here to talk with us.

So do I God. I do my best to tell you what he thought.

I'm getting hungry. Can we eat a cucumber and some figs?

But first we'll ask them if they want to be eaten.

But they can't talk...

If they could, what do you think they would say?

God and Mary both laughed and went inside to prepare some food.

LV

One day God was alone in the house. Sunlight was flowing in through the open door. He sensed something move in the corner of the room near the table where he and his mother ate. He approached it and saw that it was a baby lizard. The animal scurried against the wall and frantically began to climb. It fell back and tried to hide in a corner. God would never harm a lizard or any small animal, but the lizard did not know this. It appeared petrified with fear. God wanted to pick it up so that he could put it outside and set it free. What would happen outside? Would it get eaten by a bird or a larger animal? What would it kill to eat and survive? God was not able to catch it with his fingers. It slipped away every time. Finally he began to "guide" it towards the door. With his cupped hands he was able to alter its direction as it moved about frenetically. God was relieved when it finally ran out the door. *Have I done something good?* he wondered. *How long will the lizard survive outside in the world? Maybe I should have tried to keep it in the house. Maybe I should have protected it…*

God was perplexed. How did one know what one should do?

LVI

After the lizard had left the room, God went to work on a pair of shoes for a Roman soldier. While he worked his mind was still on the question that was so central to him: *How should one live?* When he looked around at the world, it seemed that most people did not think excessively about this question. People rarely talked deeply about the moral quandary, the quagmire of "right" and "wrong." Most people just lived. Donkeys didn't ask themselves how they should live – whether or not they should bay loudly or softly, walk fast or slowly, kick someone in the leg or butt. No, they just lived. It seemed most Jews and Romans were the same: the Jews did what Jews do and the Romans did what Romans do. They didn't ask many questions. If they did, they seemed satisfied with simple or paltry answers. They didn't search their souls. If they did, their souls were not very fertile gardens. — But some people were much more agreeable than others. *Had they decided to be nice? Or was it just their characters? Was it just the way they were? And the people who were unkind or unpleasant? Had they searched their hearts and decided to be that way? How much decision-making actually went into the way people were?*

God thought and God wondered.

He finished the shoes, drank some wine, and lay down on his bed. The sun was low, but Mary was still at the marketplace. His mind continued to wander. He couldn't put chains on it and keep it from wandering. It ran where it wanted to run. His mind was not a prison. Perhaps it was a prisoner run free…

The lizard: *Where did it come from? Did it have a purpose in life? How long would it live? Would any other lizard or creature care when it died? Would I have made its life better had I kept it in the house? How long before it gets eaten by another animal? Why is this world so cruel? Why should I care about a lizard? — The man Paul keeps telling me that my father was the son of Jehovah and that he has been resurrected from the dead and is now in Heaven. I have seen nothing dead come back to life. Why would Jehovah suddenly choose my father to be the first to come back to life? What about all the people who died before him? Didn't Jehovah care about them? — My mother tells me that Jesus would often look at the sky and shudder. His whole body would tingle as he felt the mystery... the mystery of it all... All... ALL. She says the only thing that held him to the earth was their love. I am beginning to be like my father. I am in a constant state of wonderment. When I walk outside and look at people and what they do and how they spend their time on this earth, I think, "They are so similar to animals, herd animals, except whereas birds fly and lizards crawl, they walk on two feet". I am one of them. Do this, do that. Follow this, follow that... Why? Why? What should I, God Magdalene Christ, follow? Who should I follow? How should I spend the time that I have from now until my death? Is there a "good" way to live? How does one know when one is being "good?" And good to whom? Should others count more than me? Should people count more than animals? Should the Jews count more than the Romans? Should I let Paul tell lies about my father? Should I try to stop him?*

Should I shut him up forever? Should I just shut my mouth and follow the laws of the Jews when I am with the Jews and the Romans when they wield the power? Or should I, God, create my own laws? Should I be a law unto myself? Should I want followers like Paul does? Mother says that Jesus followed nobody and wanted no followers. Should I try to prevent Paul from making a religion based on my father? Maybe a religion based on my father would be better than what the Jews or Romans have to offer… But Paul and his friends are distorting my father! They are turning what he said inside out! They are crucifying him a second time!

Just then God heard Mary's footsteps outside the door. When she entered the house there was enough light such that he could see that she was crying.

LVII

But in a sense, they were tears of joy.

Why are you crying, Mother? God's long body was spread across the blanket on his bed. Mary came and sat beside him.

I was thinking about your father.

So was I… What were you thinking about?

The day he died… According to the Julian calendar, it was exactly seventeen years ago.

God said nothing.

I think I have told you that I was the last person there, at the foot of the cross. Paul and the others had left hours before when Jesus stopped talking. I slept curled in this blanket against the wooden plank with you in my belly. It was the longest night of my life. In a sense, you saved me God. The last drops of blood of the man I loved were dripping from above me. You were inside me. Our baby. The creation of a dead man and a living woman. I hated the world. I wanted to follow Jesus to the grave. I wanted to ask a Roman soldier to run his sword through my gut. But you were there. I hated the world outside of me, but I loved what was inside of me.

O Mother…

You cannot imagine the emotion I felt that night. All of me wanted to die and all of me wanted to live. To die with the man I loved… To live with the baby inside of me…

God whispered, *How can the world be so cruel?*

Mary answered, *How can the world provide so much love? I felt both emotions at the same time. Can you imagine, dear God, all the beauty and all the ugliness at the same moment? You cannot know how I felt until you love someone like I loved your father…*

Maybe it will never happen. Maybe I will never find such love.

My greatest prayer is that you do.

But you never pray, Mother…

Life is a prayer… every day… every moment…

A prayer to whom?

To oneself and those one loves and cares about.

But didn't my father care about all life?

Yes, he did. And his prayer was always for every living creature. But he knew it was hopeless. He knew there was no one to answer his prayer. In the end, he said love was the only divinity.

Is that what he talked about before he died?

Really God, he talked about what he always talked about… loving the world, this world, the only world we have… He talked about the great unfathomable mystery of this world… He talked about the innocence of all creation… He said even his killers were innocent in that they could not help being the fools that they were… But more than anything else, he talked about how much he loved me and how lucky we were to have met. Without each other, we never would have known what love is.

And I would never have known what life is…

They were both talking through tears.

God, my darling son, in the end, what is "life?" Isn't "life" different for everyone. Doesn't every creature live living in its own unique way… This is why love is so rare. This is why your father and I loved each other so much… Because he was the one person on earth who made me feel that I was not alone. He and I had similar eyes, ears, and thoughts. Our bodies and minds never felt separate. And O how I loved him and how he loved me. Sometimes it was almost as if when I loved him I was loving myself, and in loving myself I was loving the world, and loving the world always brought me back to loving him. It was a huge cycle… one that neither of us could stop.

You saved each other…

Yes, you could say that. God, the world gives you every reason to go crazy all the time. Every day. Every night. But love gives a reason to stay sane. First I had Jesus to love, now I have you. Now you have me and one day you will find the woman with whom the world can be made beautiful.

And if I don't…

Then you will be the opposite of me: I had no love with a mother, but I had love with a man; you will have had love with a mother, but never with a woman…

O mother…

The room was silent for a period of time that no one measured. God's eyes closed just as Mary kissed him on the forehead.

LVIII

God began to wander more and work less. The money he brought in for his shoes was not essential to their survival. There was enough food in the garden for them to eat and Mary sold the excess at the marketplace. He would usually work for a few hours in the morning, then prepare a sack with a little food and drink and set off for the hills and orchards. Sometimes he would meet Joshua, but most of the time he walked alone. There was an old man who tended sheep outside of Nazareth with whom he had become friends. He didn't know the man's name nor did the man know his. But it didn't matter. Why would it matter? Sometimes the sun went halfway across the sky while they walked and talked.

For a few days Mary didn't feel well and stayed in bed. God nursed her and went himself to the marketplace to sell the vegetables. When she was better, God went back to wandering in the afternoons. He met the old man…

Ah, there you are. I haven't seen you for a while.

No, my mother was a bit ill and I had to take the vegetables to the marketplace. But she is better now.

What was it?

I don't know. She was tired and said her blood felt heavy. Blood is one of the strangest things on Earth.

Not really, actually. It's no stranger than bones or skin or teeth or the moon when it gets cut in half.

Where does blood come from?

Where does water come from? Where does your tongue come from? Where do these sheep come from…? When I kill a sheep and watch the blood pour from its body, I always think that men and sheep have much in common. Life can be taken away so easily. We both have blood that the blade of a knife can drain from our bodies and in a matter of minutes we are dead.

When you kill a sheep, do you look inside at the rest of the body? What is in there? Are there parts that serve no purpose, or does everything seem to do something to keep us alive?

I don't know. But the insides of a man and the insides of a sheep are not that different.

You have seen dead men cut open?

A few times.

And are their insides similar to those of a sheep?

Yes.

Is one more complicated than the other?

That is hard to say. Is the moon more complicated than the sun? Is a fig more complicated than a rock? Is a serpent more complicated than Herod? How to judge? How to know what things are really made of?

Isn't the life of a man more complicated than that of a fig or a sheep?

I don't know. Sometimes I think it is useless to talk about things being simple or complicated. If everything is part of the same universe, then perhaps everything shares certain qualities of "existence." Then other times I think everything is different… that every existing thing is a universe unto itself and that there is no real way to compare different parts. I don't know.

Does anyone know?

Many pretend to…

There was a moment of silence and then God said:

Do you know you have become kind of a father to me? I never knew my father as he died before I was born.

Better your father than your mother, the shepherd chuckled… *She would have taken you with her into the world of the dead.*

Yes.

Do you know who your father was?

Yes, that I do. His name was Jesus… Jesus of Nazareth. Maybe you have heard of him. Some people still talk about him even though he has been dead for seventeen years.

No, I don't know him. I rarely go to the marketplace. Other than you, my friend, I talk exclusively with my sheep. How did your father die?

Nailed to a cross like many common criminals. Pontius Pilate sentenced him to death for disturbing the peace in the land.

What did he do? Was he a violent man?

Absolutely not. He was as gentle as your lambs. At least that is what my mother says.

Then how did he disturb the peace?

Some people spread the rumour that he claimed to be the son of Jehovah and that people should follow him instead of the Romans and Jews.

And did he make such a claim?

No, to the contrary. My mother says he did not even believe in the Jewish god Jehovah. He did not believe in any gods… not the Roman gods, the Greek gods, or the Jewish god. He saw no proof of any divinity. He did not have an explanation for where the world came from. He thought it was all a great mystery.

He could have been my friend. The more I stare at the hills and sky, the more I am filled with wonder. What I have learned is that men are just like sheep… They have to follow somebody. They need a master. There are few masters and many sheep.

My father wanted no followers. He wanted people to think for themselves. He asked many questions and gave few answers. But then a man named Paul started saying that he was the son of Jehovah and that when he spoke, he spoke the word of Almighty God.

The Romans and the Jews certainly must not have liked that.

They didn't. He was judged a troublemaker and the Romans crucified him. And then, after he died, this man Paul claimed he was "resurrected", had gone to his Father in Heaven, and that he had died for the sins of mankind. Can you imagine that? My father never talked about "sin" in his life. He never talked about Jehovah. He never talked about Heaven. The only thing he talked about was respecting life and loving the world and each other. According to my mother, he loved her with every drop of blood in his body. And she loved him equally.

They were lucky to have had love. It is so rare. And you were lucky to be the fruit of the tree of their love. Most of us are the fruit of another kind of tree, a tree of random haphazard coupling.

Sometimes I think everything is random and haphazard.

I like to think not. But maybe it is so. Whenever I must choose a sheep to kill my mind says, "Why should this one die and not that one?" And there is no answer.

Do you think life is as precious to sheep as it is to men?

I don't know. I don't know what goes on in the mind of a sheep. But I do know that most men do not act as if life is precious at all. They treat it with so little respect. They kill animals and each other without a thought.

I think that was really my father's message: love life and respect life.

But what is "life?" Each man has his own

definition…

And maybe each sheep does too.

You have an interesting mind, my friend… So tell me, what do you do in this life to have money to eat?

I make shoes. I usually work in the morning then walk in the afternoon.

The old man looked at God's feet. Can you make me a pair of shoes like those you are wearing? I have a little money. I can pay you. They will be my last shoes before I die.

One never knows when death will come, except when one is nailed to a cross.

It is such a barbaric practice. For some things the Romans are civilised. For others they are ugly beasts.

God and the old man's eyes met, then God looked at the sky.

The sun is getting low. I must be going.
Yes, and come back soon.
I will. With your shoes.

God knelt down on the ground and opened his hand wide to measure the length of the old man's feet.

I will start on them tomorrow.
Thank you, my friend.
Goodbye. Till we meet again.
Yes, till we meet again.

LIX

Mary noticed that her son was not as happy as he used to be. As a child the world had been God's playground. All things were to be enjoyed. The earth and his mind were weightless. Now Mary sensed that God, like his father before him, needed to be careful lest he go crazy. She too had almost gone crazy. The problem – the equation – is really not that complicated:

If you truly care about creatures (human beings included) other than yourself, if you truly try to put yourself in other creatures' shoes even knowing all the while that this is impossible, if you understand that every creature is the centre of its own universe, if you give "value" to all other creatures knowing all the while that there is no "equality" among them, if when you see a dead creature your body cringes because you see and feel that a whole universe has died (each creature being a universe unto itself), if you believe large and small mean nothing when it comes to the value of a creature, if when you see a dead creature you imagine the tragedy and suffering before death, if when you share in the suffering you are not just thinking about your own condition of suffering and feeling sorry for yourself (like people often do when they cry at funerals, not because they are sad for the person in the coffin and that person's surviving loved ones, but because they are thinking about their own eventual death), if you think the world never has been and never will be a "fair" and "just" place, if you do not believe there is some divine hand that is guiding the universe and will eventually "take care of things" and make sure some kind of heavenly justice is served, if you think all things are simply "there" (neither divine nor superfluous), if you doubt that your eyes see "reality", if you think every moment and every "thing" is infinitely complex, if you do not believe in a creator or a creation because you think that such an idea just begs a question, if you think the human mind might very well be incapable of knowing truth, if you think the idea of truth is more than likely a human invention that has nothing to do with the world, if you think that Being simply is and always has been and always will be, if you think that nothing can be other than what it is, if you think there is no such thing as freedom of the will, if you understand that every second there is tragedy and suffering and death somewhere, if when you look at the sky you understand that there is no up or down in the universe, if you sense that the earth is a tiny speck in what is probably finitely infinite space… then insanity is a real possibility.

But so is love…

Mary knew this. She knew that someone as sensitive and thinking as God could easily go off at the deep end. She knew that love had kept her and Jesus from going crazy. Their love for each other had allowed them to stay afloat on the vast sea of wonder, horror, pain, joy, beauty, solitude, ugliness, uncertainty, suffering, ecstasy and mystery that is existence. The chariot of their love carried them across all the mountains, deserts, valleys, oceans, pits and fires of the world until Jesus was nailed to the cross. When the Roman soldiers came the next morning and Mary watched them take down the cross and detach the body of the man she loved, she did not go crazy because she had God in her belly. Now it was her turn to help God.

LX

For a moment, let us imagine that God did not live around the time of Jesus, but rather at the beginning of the 21st century. Let us imagine he was born in some corner of Western civilisation (even Nazareth today could probably fit our purposes). God would most certainly have a television, an iPhone or iPad and a computer and would spend close to half his day in front of a screen. He would constantly be bombarded by text messages, tweets, emails, phone calls, and millions of images and words. There would also be school to worry about, a huge variety of music to listen to (though "pop" and "hip-hop" would probably have the upper hand) decisions to make about what clothes to wear, what to put in one's body, and what other bodies to spend time with. God then and God today would likely be two very different Gods. Or would they? Would one God be kinder? Would one God be more reflective? Would one God be his own man? (Is it possible to be your own man at any stage in "history?") Would one God be closer to other men? Would one God ask more questions? Would one have fewer answers? Would one be more capable of love? — Normally we think of God as being outside of time and space, outside of "culture", outside "the world", outside of a context, outside of "history." But is this fair to God? Is it fair to any part of the universe to think that it is somehow not part of the universe? Is it possible for even a thinking God to have one thought that is not somehow conditioned by the world? Is it possible for a mind to think outside the world if that mind is part of the world? — Maybe this is where the idea of "a soul" came from – from a human craving and longing to get away from the world – "O please dear Lord, free me from the suffering and toil of this life! … There must be more than this body and this decaying flesh! … There must be more to my humanness! … There must be a "spirit", a "soul" that is outside the rubble of this earth! … There has to be something better than this…body!" But our God has a body and he lives in time and space. Whether he is the son of Jesus and Mary in Nazareth or the son of Mr. and Mrs. James P. Coleman in New York City, in either case he has a so-called body and a so-called mind that must carry him through "life". And God wonders what makes his body move and what makes his mind decide. What pushes him to say this or that, to go here or there, to listen to this or that music, wear these or those clothes, to accept or to question, to love or to hate, to follow or to lead? Is he "free"? Is any piece of the universe – human, godly or otherwise – actually free to think or do anything separate from "the universe"? Is not every piece of the universe built into the universe? Surely nature is not separate and free, so why would God be? — God is trying to be free. This is why we have named him God. He is trying to make sense of the whole bag of beans in his own way. He is trying to live his own life and not a life imposed on him by the world. But he has the intelligence, honesty, and courage to wonder if it is possible. He knows that most men and animals are prisoners of their bodies and minds and the culture that surrounds them. He knows it is very possible that all being is a prisoner of Being and that there are no gods or moral imperatives, and that living and dying are not part of any "plan". And he knows that if such is the case, he has no choice but to make his own way. He must become God. Now. Before it is too late.

LXI

A few days after his last talk with the old man, his mother wasn't feeling well again.

I don't think I can go to the market today, God.

It's okay, I can go. I will quickly finish a pair of shoes I am making for the old man, and then I will go sell the vegetables.

They can wait until tomorrow.

No, I'll go. Then in the afternoon I will take the shoes to the old man.

I'm just feeling tired. My body only wants to sleep.

What do you think is wrong, Mother?

Maybe I am just getting old.

You are not old.

Either I'm getting old for the world or the world is getting old for me. Death should come when one is tired of the world.

Mother, I will make a fire and give you some tea. That will help.

Thank you, my son.

God made the tea, finished the shoes, and went to the market wondering what life would be like without his mother. He had never truly imagined the thought before. He had never "felt" the idea that one day Mary would no longer be there when he came home. She was like his bed. It would always be there. As long as their little house was there, his bed would be there… and his mother would be there! But no! O God! Mothers die! Beds don't die! Mothers die! All mothers die!

God's spine went cold at the thought.

LXII

Joshua found God at the marketplace.

I went to your house expecting to find you, but I found your mother. She doesn't look well, God.

She's tired. Her life has not been easy. But then again, whose life is easy?

That is a very good question. I think life is easiest for people who forget they are alive. They are so busy with their lives that they never wonder about anything, never question anything, never doubt anything, and never really think about anything. Marcus tells me that is the way a lot of soldiers are. They just kill or get killed. They never ask why they are fighting, why they are killing, or why someone is trying to kill them. They are machines, not men.

Aren't most men machines, Joshua?

Probably. Look at the Jews. They all think the same. It makes life simple.

Do you talk to Marcus often? Have you decided he is your father?

We have both decided he is my father.

That's good.

But God, I want to talk to you about your father. This man Paul is really using him. And people are starting to believe him. Even some Jews are listening to his nonsense.

Yes, I know. What have you heard him saying?

He is promising eternal life in Heaven for everyone who is baptised in the river and who follows him and his friends John, Luke, and Matthew. He is calling himself a "Christian" and saying that Jesus Christ was the son of Jehovah and came on Earth to save the world.

What he says has nothing to do with what my father, Jesus Christ, said and believed. Paul is just another lost soul trying to find a place for himself, trying to be important, and trying to turn life into something that it is not. Were my father alive he would laugh at such babble… Actually he wouldn't laugh, he probably would have felt empathy for his friend

Paul… another weak man who needs crutches to walk through life.

But he is not alive to defend himself. He is not alive to tell people that what Paul is saying is a pile of lies.

Maybe the Romans will kill Paul for disturbing the peace.

I think even some of the Romans are starting to listen to him.

What an absurd irony. First they kill my father and then they worship him!

I hear some Romans saying they have too many gods. It is easier to have just one.

People will believe anything. The longer I live the crazier the world looks.

For me too.

Are you hungry? Here, have some figs. I will never sell them all today. I brought too many. And besides, I must take a pair of shoes to an old man outside of town. He's a shepherd… In fact, why don't you come with me. He's an interesting man. He has become kind of like my father…

Now we both have fathers…

They laughed and together went to see the old man and his sheep.

LXIII

I see you have a friend with you today.

He's really my only friend, except for you and my mother.

Your friend will be my friend. How is your mother?

She's not feeling so well again. I went to the market in her place this morning. But I finished your shoes first. Here they are.

How wonderful. I have not had shoes for years. My feet have been my shoes, like the feet of my sheep. Let me try them and see if they fit on the beaten feet of an old man… Ah, yes… Thank you so much.

It is my pleasure to make shoes for friends.

I have some coins to give you. They have been with me for weeks, since I killed and sold the meat of one of my animals.

The old man pulled money from a pocket.

I do not need nor want your denarii.

Then give them to your friend or your mother.

Give them to your sheep.

What can my sheep do with money?

They can buy shoes…

The old man laughed, then he took a few steps in his new shoes.

It's odd to have something between my feet and the ground. With shoes, one doesn't know what one is stepping on.

Animals always do.

But they don't see what they step on in the same way we do. They don't differentiate between "rocks", "dirt", "mud", and "grass", like we do. They live in a different world. I'm not sure which world, but I'm sure their world is very different from yours and mine. What fascinates me is how they will follow me wherever I go. For years… for their whole lives they will follow me.

That is not so different from people. Look at the Jews following their rabbis and the Romans following their leaders.

You are right. There is little difference.

I wonder how big the world is and how many

different things there are that people follow. All we know are the Jews and the Romans, but maybe there are other peoples with other ideas all over the world. Maybe there are even "free" people who have no rabbis or Roman generals to follow.

I doubt it, but who knows?

What is the world, anyway? We talk about it, but no one knows what it is. We walk on it, but we don't know what is under the ground. No one has been to the end of the world. No one knows if it has an end. Maybe it goes on forever.

I have spent my life here with sheep. My father had sheep. His father had sheep. Beyond that I know nothing.

And I have spent my life around Nazareth. The farthest I have been is maybe walking three hours. Then I came back home. The Romans have come from Rome. But where is that? I have no idea. You have no idea. How can anyone who has never been there have any idea?

What amazes me is how little we know about anything, yet people are satisfied with the paltry answers they have. We have absolutely no idea about where the world came from, how it works, where it is going, how man and animals and everything else got *here, how our minds and bodies function, what is in our blood, how we breathe and think and decide… yet everybody acts like they are "at home" in the world, like they have their "place" in the world, like the world makes sense. But "sense"? What is "sense"? It is the same for sheep. Look at them… They feel like the whole universe is in its proper place.*

As long as they have grass to chew on and water to drink.

Yes. Look at what men need. Food, wine, a bed, someone to follow, companionship…

We are simple creatures.

But some of us are simpler than others. Some are more complicated. Some are not satisfied with the answers…

Just like some sheep that baa louder than others. Some even try to run away from the herd.

Yes, it is the same with men.

I don't think I can ever be satisfied with what a rabbi or Roman tells me about anything.

Nor a Greek…

Nor anyone… even myself. My mind will never be satisfied. Even with itself.

Do you think a mind can fuse with another mind?

It is rare, but I see no reason why it can't happen.

You said your mother and father had fused before he was killed on the cross.

Yes, that is what my mother told me.

So why would fusing with another person be desirable? That is a question I cannot answer because it has never happened to me. If I have fused with anything it is with my sheep.

My mother says one doesn't know what it is until it happens. It is what the world calls "love".

But maybe it is not a "thing," maybe it is never the same from two lovers to the next, maybe every love is as different as the sun and the moon.

We don't even know what the sun and moon are.

No, we don't.

We know so little about anything.

You know, I have been tending sheep my whole life. Compared to most lives it has been long. I am old. Most people can never say that. I have had more time to think than the majority of people who visit the earth.

Why do you say, "visit the earth"?

Isn't that what it is? A visit is when you go someplace and don't stay. That is what we all do in this world. Perhaps if you think of life as a visit, you will feel it differently… So let me tell you about one of my favourite thoughts. I say "favourite" because it is

*one that comes to me often. It is a thought that makes
me want to laugh and cry at the same time.*

Aren't those the best kind of thoughts?

Certainly.

So tell us your thought…

*It is this: I will use myself as the example. Oneself is
what one should know best, but that might not be true
at all. But it doesn't matter in this case — in the case
of my thought… So here it is: I ask myself,* "What is
your origin? Where do you come from? How did
you get here? How did you come to be?" *Now of
course you can ask the same questions for absolutely
everything that exists, but for now we will only ask it
for me.*

It is a very good question.

*So let us look at the answer… Maybe I should say
let us look* for *the answer because it is possible we won't
find an answer to look at… But let us look. For me to
be in this world, my mother and father had to have
been in this world and had to have come together to
make me. They are the only two people I ever saw that
have to do with my existing. I never saw their parents
who had to exist for me to exist. They were long dead
before I was born. But think… their parents had their
own parents and their parents' parents had their own*

parents, and on and on and on… But back to when? That is the question nobody asks or thinks about. Back to when? For every single person who is in the ancestral line of my existence, there had to have been two parents to make him or her… No one just "appeared" out of nowhere. At least, I don't think they did.

I don't either…

So… so… do you see what I am saying… or thinking? My existence goes back forever and ever. It makes no sense to think I had "a beginning". And now is when I laugh… Everything else that exists is the same. Nothing – absolutely nothing – "had a beginning!" Everything goes back forever! You, your friend, those sheep, the sun, the moon, the pebbles under my new shoes… Everything! And now I cry! What does this mean? It means there is no origin of anything! We can never know the origin of anything because there is no origin to anything because everything goes back forever and ever and ever! Everything… forever! This is the thought of the old man with the sheep…

I wonder if anyone else has ever had this thought?

I don't know. It doesn't matter. If they have, then I have a friend.

It is a beautiful thought.

I am just glad to have been able to tell it to someone. I have had it for a long time, but I have had no one to share it with because everyone else will just start telling me about Jehovah or the Roman or Greek gods that supposedly "created everything"! The same old tired answers are immediately always given. But my thought is not old and tired. It is lovely and frightening at the same time.

It is almost not "human"…

Actually when I have it, it makes me dizzy.

But sometimes it is good to be dizzy.

As long as you can settle back to the earth… O the earth! O what a place! What a wonder!

There was a silence even among the sheep. God, Joshua, and the old man could all hear themselves breathing. Finally God said he should to be going to see how his mother was feeling.

Come back soon. It is nice to have some company.

We will.

And maybe it's time you started looking for a little of that love we talked about.

Can one look for it?

I don't know. I've never known what it is.

Maybe it is not too late.

I'm as old as your grandfathers.

The ones I never knew. The only person tied to me that I have known is my mother. But in a sense, you are the father I never knew.

And you are the son I never had.

Now you have two…

We are as silly as the sheep.

Sillier perhaps.

They need me. I need thee.

Every hour…

Thank you for the shoes.

Thank you for the thoughts.

Till we meet again…

Yes, till we meet again…

LXIV

Spring passed, the days lingered, the olives grew, the donkeys bayed in the morning but were quiet at the end of the day as the heat sapped their energy. There was relative peace in the area of Palestine. As long as they obeyed the laws, the Romans basically left the Jews alone to live and worship as they pleased. God and Mary resided on the edge of the Jewish part of town, but of course they were considered "bad" Jews because they were never seen at the synagogue. Their minds had been corrupted by "the devil", the devil being the force behind all things "un-Jewish". But God and Mary were nice to people and because of this were somewhat of an enigma. How can you not worship Jehovah and still be a good person? But not only were God and Mary good to others, they did not try to force their "disbeliefs" or doubts on others. They let the Jews be Jews and respected them in their beliefs and practices. They just did not share their view of the world for a thousand reasons.

One thing, however, was certain: No Jewish parents wanted their daughter to consider marrying a man like God. No… no… and no! A Jewish girl was not to marry a man who did not follow the laws of the Torah!

But children do not always do what their parents want. Even two thousand years ago – eighteen years after the death of Jesus Christ – there were boys and girls going against the will of their parents. God, of course, was not one of them as his relationship with his mother was such that he had nothing to rebel against. They loved and respected each other and they shared the same doubts about what was considered "truth". God questioned all the values and beliefs of the world around him. That was enough…

Naomi, however, was a very different story. By the time she had her first menstrual period she was at war with her parents, particularly her father. Initially it had not been an open war. It had been silent and private. She was the third offspring in a devoutly Jewish family of five children. For years she kept her ideas to herself. When the family repeated the same prayers before every meal, she thought it was ridiculous. Was Jehovah deaf? Couldn't He remember they had prayed a few hours before? Why did they have to say the same things a thousand times? When a lamb was sacrificed on the day of the Passover, she thought it was barbaric. Why would God want innocent animals killed in His name? She watched her parents choose a man for her older sister to marry. Her sister didn't love the man and Naomi thought the man had no more character than a rag with which one dries one's face. He never thought for himself. He only followed traditions. How could her sister spend her life with such a boring man?

When it was Naomi's turn to have a husband, the war became open. She could stay silent no more. She wanted her own man or no man. She could not let her father choose a husband for her. That was impossible! Her body told her it was impossible. Her mind told her it was impossible. Her whole being told her it was impossible. Where is it written in this universe, she thought, that a girl should be required to spend her life on Earth with a man she doesn't love, especially a man that she has not chosen herself?

When she was sixteen Naomi saw two possibilities: she could run away or she could go crazy. But where could she run to? She knew that girls alone in the world quickly became slaves or victims of cruel unsavoury men. She knew that if she ran away she would likely be shortening her life. But what life? She couldn't live "the life" that her parents had planned for her. She looked at her body: *I cannot share this with a man I don't love.* She looked into her mind: *I cannot spend my life with a man that I cannot talk to and with whom I have nothing in common.*

She thought of killing herself. Other girls had done so.

But fortunately, before she ran too far away or killed herself, she met God, not the invisible God of many so-called "holy" books, but God the man with flesh and blood, the beloved son of Mary Magdalene and Jesus Christ.

Miraculously or not, God saved Naomi and Naomi saved God.

LXV

Their meeting was like all meetings. The infinite circumstances of their lives had led them to be in the same place at the same time. This happens every day to essentially everyone. You go somewhere and there are other human beings. You meet some. But what doesn't happen every day is that you fall in love with one of them. No one calls it fate when you don't fall in love. No one talks about destiny or things being meant to be with regard to the thousands of people you meet that you don't care about in any special way. But when you do meet someone and fall in love, many people want to call it the work of fate, destiny, God, gods, cosmic design, or some other such term. Or, on the other side of the intellectual fence, there are those who want to say that such happenings – even all happenings – are random, chance, the luck of the dice… But what if neither is the case? What if neither destiny nor chance has anything to do with the world? What if these are just human terms to try to explain things to the insecure human head? What if everything just *is*? What if there is no god or purpose behind anything? And what if there is no random chaos either? What if all being – the entire universe, the totality of all existence – just *exists*? Then what do we call the meeting of God and Naomi…?

Naomi had run away. Not far, not forever. Just away. The night before, her father had told her that the Holy Spirit had destined her to marry Isaac. She responded that Isaac meant less to her than the family donkey. She wouldn't do it. She would die first. Her father ordered her to get down on her knees, pray to Jehovah, and repent her multitude of sins. She refused. He screamed at her. She was a "sinner"! She was "evil"! The devil had taken her! She would "rot in hell"! Her head and body were on fire. She ran for the door and her father was not able to catch her. She fled to the olive orchard on the hill where she spent the night. Fortunately, it was summer.

Mary was feeling a little better, but God had helped her take the vegetables to the marketplace in the early morning. When the stand was ready for business, he left his mother and went for a long walk and thought about everything and nothing. On the hill in the orchard sitting next to a tree was a girl. She seemed to be sobbing. God wasn't sure of that until he got closer.

Hello…

She did not look at him.

Hello…

The eyes furtively glanced his way, then she buried her face in her hands. God knelt down next to her and spoke softly.

I do not think I know you. Have we ever met before?

The girl said nothing but sensed that the voice certainly meant no harm.

May I sit here for a moment? If I am bothering you, if you want me to go away, I will leave like the stars in the morning.

Minutes passed. Neither said anything. The sobs became less frequent. Finally it was the girl who spoke.

I saw lots of stars this night. I didn't know there were so many stars.

You slept here?

I didn't sleep much, but I was here.

Do you have no home?

I have a home where I no longer want to go.

Why is that?

There is nothing for me there.

Are your parents dead?

No, I am dead.

God tried to imagine what she meant. He looked at the girl's bare feet.

I am a shoemaker. If you have no shoes, I could make you some.

I have shoes. I just didn't have them on when I ran out the door.

You ran away?

Yes.

Last night?

Yes.

Do you want to tell me what you ran away from?

From a father who insists that I marry a man for whom I have no love.

Love is rare inside and outside of marriage.

Not only do I have no love for this man, but, like I told my father, I have no more feeling for him than for a donkey.

Maybe it is easier to love a donkey than a man.

I wouldn't know. I have never loved either. We have no donkey and...

She didn't finish her sentence.

I imagine your father and your father's father and your father's father's father are all Jews. Your father wants you to marry a Jew. You must marry a Jew...

I wouldn't mind marrying a Jew if I could find one I loved.

Maybe if you got to know the man your father wants you to marry you would love him.

Who knows? Anyway, Jews don't care about love in marriage. They care about God. They are really married to their God... Jehovah. Their love for Him is all that counts.

And it's not that way for you?

How can I love God? I have no idea if He is real or not. I have prayed to Him a thousand times and never had an answer.

The same thing happened to me.

Are you Jewish?

Not really. My ancestors were, but I have no reason

to believe that the Jews have more truth than the Romans.

Your parents don't force you to believe things?

No. My mother is like me.

My parents force everything on me. Not just marriage. They want me to believe everything they believe. They want me to see the world exactly the way they see it. But that is ridiculous. Are we supposed to be exactly like our parents? Why can't they accept that I am different?

Because they think they have the truth.

Then it is a bad truth. No good truth would force a daughter to marry a man she didn't love. For them I am a black sheep in a family of white swans.

A black sheep can be as beautiful as a white swan.

Not according to my parents. They think I am the devil...

Have you tried to talk to them?

Of course I have. But they won't listen. Their minds are closed doors that never let in any fresh air. They don't think. They just follow the rabbis.

Maybe it is better if one doesn't think. People who don't think are often happy in their simple worlds. Maybe it is best for them to stay there.

I don't care if they stay there, but they should not

force me to stay there with them. They cannot imagine that I am not made like they are and that I want a different life.

What life do you want?

I don't know. How could I know? I've been locked in my parents' cage for sixteen years. I've seen nothing else. I just know I don't want their life… She looks at God's face… *Tell me, do you believe in Hell?*

No, I don't. I cannot imagine Jehovah being that cruel. But maybe he is.

Do you think he would send someone to Hell for not being a Jew?

I can't believe he would ever punish someone who thought deeply and followed the dictates of his own conscience.

Maybe Jehovah is not just. Maybe he is cruel. Maybe he is like my father.

It is a possibility. Anything is possible. For me, the world is a great mystery. The older I get, the greater the mystery.

They were both silent. Both were staring into the orchard. Finally their heads turned and their eyes met. The son of Jesus and Mary smiled and spoke.

*We have talked all this time and we don't know
each other's name. What is yours?*
Naomi. And you?
God.
God...? O my God!

Both laughed and Naomi's weary head fell into
God's lap.

LXVI

Mary was sitting up in bed. God was at her side. He took her hand and rubbed it.

Mother, today I met a girl... a woman.
Where did you meet her?
In the olive orchard.
How old is she?
Sixteen.
I think this is the first time in your life that you have come home and said, "Mother, I met a girl..."
It is the first time in my life that I have felt like this.
Like what...? You don't have to tell me. I can see it in your eyes.
I was taking my walk and I found her crying, sobbing under a tree.

Why? Let me guess? She is being forced to marry…

How did you know?

It is the tragic tradition in Judea. Our world does not know how to accommodate the human heart. Women are slaves to the civilisation.

Aren't men also?

Yes, but in a different way. Women are there to keep the species alive. Men are there to decide who has power over the species.

You were never forced to marry. You were lucky.

I was not forced to marry because I had no parents who wanted me to uphold a family tradition. I had no family and no tradition. I was not forced to marry a man, but men forced me to do other things many times. I was only trying to survive…

And you never had a baby with those other men?

That is the miracle of my life. Only with your father – the only man I ever loved – did I produce a baby. You, dear God, are the apple that fell from the tree of the greatest love on Earth. For that you are the luckiest man and I am the luckiest woman. So who is this girl you met in the orchard?

Before I tell you, tell me how you are feeling. How was the day?

I sold all the vegetables quickly, then I came back

home to bed. My body just feels tired all the time. It is as if my arms and legs are ten times their normal weight and I must drag them around wherever I go.

O Mother, I know you will get better…

No, you don't know that. The only thing you know is that one day life will be sucked out of my body…

Mother…

God, one day I will die…

Yes, but…

It will happen when it happens

But not now… not yet…

Isn't it better to die too early than too late?

God squeezed his mother's hand and then rubbed each of her fingers.

Now tell me about the girl. I see love in your eyes and I want to know about the spark that started the fire.

Her name is Naomi. She is very strong of mind, but her body is as delicate as any flower. She ran away from her home last night when her father became violently angry because – like you said – she refuses to marry a man she doesn't love. She does not believe in the Jewish version of life. She has no idea why we are on Earth.

But she doesn't want to be told how to live. She wants to live her own life.

That is very hard to do in this world. Few people do it. Few people even think about doing it. We are all constantly pressured to act in certain ways. If it isn't parents pressuring you to obey, it's the Romans. If it isn't the Romans, it's the rabbis. If it isn't the rabbis, it's the congregation. Who can truly live his or her own life with all the social pressures people have? Your father and I were very lucky. We were pretty much able to live on the outskirts of society. But remember, he ended up dead on a cross.

He died too early.

Maybe, but maybe not.

He didn't deserve to die.

One thing is sure — his early death left me loving him forever.

Who really killed him, Mother?

The world killed him, just like the world kills everybody else. The world listened to Paul who made false claims about Jesus. The world took the easy way out. It usually does.

Well, Naomi is not taking the easy way. She refuses to follow her parents. She refuses to follow the Torah. She says she will die before she marries a man she doesn't love. She will die before she is forced to have babies with a man she doesn't love.

Where has she gone now? Where did she go when you said goodbye. Maybe you should have brought her here.

Maybe I should have. But she said she would go home one more time and try to reason with her parents.

She is courageous to try, but rarely can you reason with people who believe they possess "eternal truth" — especially people who are worried about the fiery judgment of Jehovah and the wicked judgment of the other people in their group.

We'll see. We are meeting again tomorrow at the same time.

I would be worried that she might not be able to come. Her father might not allow her to leave the house. She ran away once. He might not let her run away again... What does she look like, God?

Like an angel dropped from Heaven.

That doesn't help. I have never seen an angel.

I have only seen one.

O my son, I'm happy for you. Do you think she loves you?

Today she fell asleep in my lap. For an hour I caressed her hair, neck, and shoulders.

And her sleeping body caressed yours…

Yes. I felt something I have never felt before. Everything about her fit perfectly into my eyes, ears, hands, and mind. I think she felt the same thing.

If you love each other, you will know. If one side feels doubt, it is not love… But let me warn you God, love is also a kind of slavery. We are slaves to the love. When I met your father, I could do nothing else but love him. It was impossible for me "not" to love him. I was a slave to him and my love for him. But I was also his master. Because he loved me madly in return, he was my slave. I could not help but follow him and he could not help but follow me. This is the great irony of love: you are both slave and master at the same time. You are enslaved by the love, but you only feel free when you are together.

O Mother…

Dear God, in one way love is the simplest thing on Earth. Either it is there or it isn't. If it is there, you will feel you are truly living only when you are together. If you love someone, there is always a hole in the world when you are apart.

I feel that hole now wanting and waiting to see her tomorrow.

Yes. Love itself is simple, but the world makes it

complicated. The world is not kind to love. It almost always has other plans. It is jealous of love. It is vengeful. People who don't have love don't like to see others who do have it. I don't think most people even know what love is. I surely didn't until I met Jesus.

I will tell you soon if I have it and know what it is.

I would love to live to see my son living to love…

With that Mary got out of bed and prepared a meal for God. She herself was able to eat very little.

LXVII

Naomi was there long before their scheduled meeting time. She had escaped the house in the middle of the night after her father had beaten her. He had thrashed her with a tree branch: three lashes for running away… three lashes for refusing to pray. That was his idea of justice. She had been in the olive grove for five hours when she finally saw God approaching.

You're already here. I thought I was early.
I ran away during the night. I've been here for a long time. I don't know how long. My father beat me yesterday. I don't know why I went home. I should have known. As soon as I walked in the house he started screaming. He threw me to the floor, bared my

back and hit me. At least now I am free. I will never go back.

There were no tears in her voice. There was only resolution.

Did he hit you with his hand?

No, I think it was a branch of a tree. It felt like a whip. But it doesn't matter now. I am gone. He will never beat me again.

But what if he finds you? He will certainly come looking for you.

I must hide, that's for sure. I must hide until he stops looking. Either that or I must run away.

She showed him the welts on her back.

It is still bleeding a little. We must go to my house. My mother said you should have come home with me yesterday.

She was right. I should have.

You can hide there and my mother can treat your back. I'm sure she has something to put on it.

Thank you, dear God. Thank you. All I want to do is get as far away as possible from the man who calls himself my father. All he has taught me is how not to live. Nothing will change him, so I must change my life. I want my mind to fly away… far away… like a bird flying to another land… Maybe it's not possible… I don't know, but I must try.

I will help you if I can.

Today it is hard to think of my father as a human being. Last night he was an uncontrollable animal. He would listen to nothing I tried to say. It was hopeless for me to argue or resist… I just wanted him to finish so I could run away.

Which direction is your house from here?

She pointed in the direction opposite from the one God had come.

That's good. We will be a decent distance from your home.

It is not my home anymore.

Do you have a scarf or any other clothes?

No. I brought nothing. I just got to the door, opened it, and ran.

My mother can give you a few things. She is home now. She didn't go to the market. She hasn't been feeling well lately.

I'm sorry.

Let's go now. If your father is looking for you, it's better for you to be in my house than out here in the open.

Yes.

Mary heard the door rattle and quickly sat up in bed.

Hello Mother. I am here with Naomi.

Hello, welcome Naomi. God has told me about you.

There is not much to tell, except that I have had to run away from my home.

Mother, her father beat her last night. The wounds on her back are still bleeding a little. Have we anything to put on them?

Yes, I will get it.

Mary rose very slowly from the bed and went to the cupboard on the other side of the room.

You must stay with us for a few days, Naomi. Do you think your father is looking for you?

Probably, but last night he told me I should rot in Hell. Maybe he's hoping the devil will accommodate me.

Nazareth is not that big. If he can't find you in a day or two, he will think you have fled to another town or perhaps have been taken by a Roman soldier. I was an orphan. I know what it is to be alone out there in Judea. Here you are safe for now.

Thank you, Mary.

Don't thank me. Thank God. He found you in the orchard yesterday.

We found each other, Mother.

Of course… Naomi, come and sit on the bed. Let me see your back.

Naomi lifted her frock and Mary applied her ointment.

So he beat you because you refuse to marry the man he has chosen for you? Is that it?

Yes, but it is more than that. I just couldn't live the way he wanted me to live. It wasn't only about marriage.

It is always more complicated than meets the eye… Naomi, your back will be better in a few days. It might be hard to sleep tonight. Did you sleep last night?

No. Or just a little in the olive orchard.

You must be exhausted. Have you eaten?

No, but…

God, lay some bread and olives on the table. And some wine. Naomi must eat and then have a little sleep. She will have my bed while she is here.

No, I wouldn't think of it.

There is no thinking to do. God will sleep with you in the large bed and I will sleep in God's bed.

You're too kind.

One is never too kind. But some people are too unhappy to accept kindness. I'm sure you are not one of these people, Naomi.

I don't think so.

Mary finished treating the girl's back. They sat at the table together and God and Naomi ate. Mary tired quickly and was soon resting on God's bed. When Naomi finally settled down for a nap, Mary, talking more to herself than to her son or his new friend, said…

God's father, Jesus, made that bed… In that bed we made God … It is the bed of the greatest love this world has ever known… Sleep my child and peace attend thee… You have suffered enough… Now it is your turn to find love… Love… O love… To know I have known you… Jesus and Mary… Mary Magdalene and Jesus Christ… One… Take me now…

But she didn't die that day. Instead she slept.

LXVIII

God closed the door with nary a sound so as not to disturb Mary. They took a lonely path away from the town toward the River Jordan. Naomi had on some of Mary's clothes and a light scarf around her head.

You are lucky, God, to have a mother like that.
I know. No one chooses his or her parents. One must try to appreciate good ones and not let bad ones destroy you. That is your challenge, Naomi. It does no good to blame the world, especially parents. Good or bad, they allowed you to be in this world. One must make due with what one has, just like with one's legs, arms, heart, and mind.
I know. Of course I know. I have left my parents

now. They will live their lives, and I will live mine.

Yes.

How far is it to the river? You don't think we're taking a risk…

No. No more of a risk than staying in the house. If your father goes to every house in Nazareth, he'll come to ours. I don't think he'll go to a place by the river that he probably doesn't even know about. I have come here a hundred times and never met anybody.

When was the last time you bathed?

A week ago. And you?

Even longer. Maybe ten days. I'm glad you had the idea to go to the river.

And it's hot. The water will feel good on our bodies. Just be careful with your back.

It is feeling better since your mother put the ointment on it. I'll be fine. You know God, my father was so angry that I thought maybe he would kill me… and I thought that in so doing he might be doing me a favour.

God did not say anything. He tried to imagine what Naomi had been through and what it would have been like to have had a violent father. God had never experienced violence. The only pain he had

had was from thinking about the suffering of others.

How much farther to the river?
Just a few minutes.
How did you find this path?
My mother showed me. She and Jesus would come
to bathe away from the crowds. She and I came many
times, but not recently… not since she has been feeling
weak.
Do you fear she will die?
We all die.

They walked the rest of the way in silence. They undressed where Mary and Jesus had. When you love someone and they take off their clothes for the first time, it makes you love them even more. In love, everything fits.

LXIX

Naomi would never know if her father had looked for her or not. They never saw each other again. He would do her no more harm. In any case, she would not stay in Judea much longer.

That evening, when God and Naomi came back from the river, Mary was up and putting food on the table. She had not worried when she awoke from her sleep and found them gone. She was too tired and weak to worry. Her only concern was setting out a few things to eat for when they got home. Darkness was near and she knew they would be there soon.

Mary sat with them at the table for a few minutes. They told her of their promenade to the river. No, they hadn't seen anybody. Yes, her back was feeling better. Yes, they had enough to eat. No, they didn't mind if she rested while they were still eating.

Mary lay down for the last time in God's bed. God and Naomi ate, talked softly, and put things away. They couldn't wait to get into the large bed in the corner of the room.

At the river they had held hands, embraced, and kissed a few times in the water. Then they dried, put their clothes back on and walked home. Now they took their clothes off for the night. Under the blanket – the same blanket Mary had had round her body at the foot of the cross on which Jesus died – God and Naomi caressed and kissed each other's body with the softest lips and the surest hands. They were both exactly where they wanted to be.

In the morning the world would have a different Pietà. God holding Mary's limp body in his arms. When God and Naomi finally finished crying, Naomi stayed in the house while God went out to find Joshua and Marcus. They helped him wrap his mother in her blanket, carry her to the olive grove, dig a hole, and bury her.

And yes, Mary died while God and Naomi were

making love.

The next day the lovers quit Judea. There was nothing left for them in the holy land. Like Chaplin and Goddard at the end of *Modern Times*, arm in arm they wandered off to see the world, possessing nothing more than the clothes on their backs and their love for life and each other. God did have a few coins that he had saved from making shoes, but he gave them to a blind woman as they walked past Herod's temple.

VOL. III

GOD &
NAOMI

In the morning the world would have a different Pietà. God holding Mary's limp body in his arms. When God and Naomi finally finished crying, Naomi stayed in the house while God went out to find Joshua and Marcus. They helped him wrap his mother in her blanket, carry her to the olive grove, dig a hole and bury her.

Yes, Mary expired while God and Naomi were making love.

The next day the lovers quit Judea. There was nothing left for them in the holy land. Like Chaplin and Goddard at the end of *Modern Times*, arm in arm they wandered off to see the world possessing nothing more than the clothes on their backs and their love for life and each other. God did have a few coins that he had saved from making shoes, but he gave them to a blind woman as they walked past Herod's temple.

In the year 18 A. D. no one had any idea how big the earth was. Today we have a similar situation in that we don't know how big the universe is. We talk about it, throw out some big numbers, but do we really know? Modern physicists tell us that if – relatively speaking - the distance between the earth and the sun is the equivalent of the point of a pencil, then the distance from the earth to the edge of the Milky Way is from Jerusalem to New York. It's that big. But beyond that, nobody really knows how far it goes, or what is out there. God and Naomi leaving Palestine was the equivalent of two astronauts today heading straight out into space, past the moon and sun, and eventually out of our galaxy. They knew Judea, the Jews, the Romans, the

Torah, and a little bit about the Greeks. But the rest of the world? … They had absolutely no idea what was out there. But they wanted to see it. Fortunately, they would live for two thousand years and hence would be able to observe quite a lot.

Like Jesus and Mary before them, God and Naomi were very curious about the world, life, and thinking. They observed how Jews and Romans differed in their beliefs about God, truth, and morality. Though they had been nurtured in a society that believed in the Old Testament, Jehovah, Moses, and the Ten Commandments, they had a hunch that there were many other ways to understand and view existence. They didn't trust the Jews, the Romans, the Bible, and especially not this man Paul who was trying to start a new religion calling God's father, Jesus, the "resurrected Son of God". In Judea they had witnessed beauty, barbarism, ingenuity, stupidity, ugliness, kindness, cruelty, savagery, tenderness, suffering, resignation, hope, hate and a few glimpses of love. Would they see more of the same as they set out to see the world? They had no idea. They just wanted to see what was out there and what was going on. And the fact that they would live for two millennia would give them an advantage over most observers of the world. The piddling thirty, fifty, seventy, or ninety years that is normally allotted to the human body and mind allows one only so much opportunity to understand existence. Of course we are all limited, but by having their terrestrial visit lengthened more than fortyfold, God and Naomi were in a good position get a decent idea of what earthly life is all about. But let's be honest… time is no guarantee of lucidity, clarity, truth, knowledge, or any such thing. As some people age their beliefs simplify and petrify, for others complexity and doubt take over. In any case, God and Naomi would stay healthy for one thousand nine hundred years. Only when the two horrendous world wars ravaged much of the earth did their bodies begin to give out. They would die together exactly two thousand years after Jesus was born. Neither wanted to live forever anyway. Both sensed that eternity might be too long. But overall they were happy to see the sun come up 730,000 times. Today the average person experiences about twenty-five thousand sunrises.

For Naomi and God to survive so long in this world of multifarious dangers and diseases, some kind of guardian angel was necessary. Travelling in the twenty-first century is hard enough, but when God and Naomi walked out of Jerusalem there were no road signs pointing their way, no "kilometre" or "mile" numbers indicating how far it was from here to there, no passports, no smiling billboards saying "Welcome to Texas" or "You are now leaving Palestine", no real borders, no cars, no stagecoaches, no buses, taxis, trains, planes, GPSs, accurate maps, Booking.coms, or travel guides. No… back then if you wanted to go somewhere you walked on your own two feet, and if you were going very far from home you had little or no idea what to expect. Travel was often perilous, with power frequently resting in the blood-stained hands of bandits and marauders. Today's world isn't perfect, but…

So what guardian angel was watching over God and Naomi as they wandered the world? Did they have some sort of divine escort? Nah… It would have been nice, but no, God and Naomi just had each other. Their *ange gardien* was simply their unflinching abiding love for life. Everywhere they went they exuded the feeling that the simple fact of being alive was a miracle in itself. And people everywhere seemed to sense this and, hence, were generally very kind to them. People immediately intuited that God and Naomi wanted nothing from others, that they posed no danger or threat to anyone, and that they simply wanted to love each other and see – and enjoy - as much of the world as they could. They didn't want to change the people and places they visited. They looked neither up nor down at humans and civilisations. They looked the world straight in the eye and accepted it for what it was, not wishing or wanting it to be something else. It was almost as if God and Naomi were invisible. They got in nobody's way and they made no judgments about what they encountered and observed. They had no pretention of benevolence or making the world a better place. They were simply kind and respectful to every creature they encountered, human and otherwise.

That first morning they decided to walk north never straying too far from the great blue sea. There was something about its openness, vastness, and mystery that was like a spark in their guts. For months they walked up and down arid hills and plains and along beaches. "Which is bigger," Naomi once asked, "the land, the sea, or the sky?" God answered with a question, "Do you think any of them end?"

One day they came upon a fertile river that emptied into the sea. They followed it eastward where they saw many Roman soldiers and masses of slaves building walls and working the land. They were near the great city of Damascus that they had heard about in the Bible. They stayed for a few days watching the bustle of humanity. "Why do people do what they do and not other 'things'?" God said one afternoon. Naomi didn't answer. She was thinking about all the pain women had endured giving birth to all the human beings passing before her eyes. She had never had a child herself, but her mother had told her how she had not cared if she lived or died as her babies were struggling to leave her womb and see the world. As she was lost in her thoughts, God said, "I watch birds blithely cruising and darting through the sky... I see men slaving under the burning sun and wonder if I should cry..."

They went back to the sea and eventually their path turned in the direction of the cooling sun. They chatted with an old man tending sheep who told them that if they kept walking they would find the rich and wonderful Hellenic kingdom, though he wasn't sure how long it would take for them to get there. He thought less than a year.

He was right. After a hundred days of ambling in relative solitude, they came upon a coterie of Roman soldiers who told them that if they kept on, in three days' time they would be able to see the Acropolis, "a building as beautiful as anything in Rome".

God and Naomi arrived in Greece long before Christianity did. They decided to settle down for a while, rest their bodies, and learn a new language. They were given a room in a small house owned by a man named Epictetus. He showed them the Acropolis and explained how the Athenian community was organised. It made God wonder if this "Zeus" creature he kept hearing about might actually be for real. "How could men build such a building?" he remarked to Naomi. "How can people be so civilised?" she replied, adding that she wasn't sure which surprised her more… man's goodness or his barbarity. (She still had scars on her back from the beatings her father had given her.)

Within months Naomi and God were able to understand and converse with the locals in the marketplace. Epictetus helped them by saying,

"Languages are not difficult to learn. Three-year-olds can speak them all. You just have to bathe in them and they will sink into your skin."

God and Naomi noticed there was much more "intellectual" discussion among the people in Hellas than there had been back in Palestine. In Palestine things were rather straightforward: the Jews followed the rabbis, the rabbis followed the Torah, and the Romans took care of governing the place. People didn't spend a lot of time worrying about metaphysical and moral questions. They were much like people today who want to have a nice house, a nice car, a big television, watch football games, have a few beers, and when it's over, go to Heaven. The rest just doesn't mean too much. In Hellas things were different. Epictetus himself had been a slave in Rome and had been banished from the city by an emperor who "hated all philosophers". He reflected constantly and insisted that people should not worry about what they can't control. "Don't grieve over spilled milk because it's already been spilled and there is absolutely nothing you can do about it except clean up the mess." He talked softly and walked gently, but he was a firm supporter of Zeus, "whose fiery breath had organised all life." He told

Naomi and God that, "We should accept Zeus's desires as the world is unfolding according to His wishes." He also gave consummate thanks to Zeus for everything because, "In the end everything belongs to Him." This amused God and Naomi as in many ways it reminded them of the people back in Palestine. Zeus and Jehovah had much in common, but neither Naomi nor God could see a reason to believe one was real and the other wasn't. How the world got here and who owned it and watched over it remained an enigma. For them, neither Jehovah not Zeus provided a sufficient answer.

They spent some of their last days in Hellas watching and listening to architects, fascinated as they were by the Greek capacity to build. God said, "If I were running the world there wouldn't be any houses and everybody would be sleeping under the stars or in caves. I have no idea how to build such structures. It's a good thing I'm not running the world." Naomi smiled and said, "But if you were running the world there wouldn't be any slaves sweating in unbearable heat." She kissed him and God wondered if she might be right.

They stayed in the Greek world from summer to

spring. The weather had been almost as warm as it was in Judea and the people went about their daily lives with a certain calm and serenity. They saw many babies born and many people die. They heard much talk about the cosmos, politics, morality, and what constituted a noble life. God often thought that, given what his mother had told him about Jesus, the father he never met would probably have liked these people. They noticed how the Hellenes treated their dead with great respect and how they believed that when a person died, his or her "spirit" immediately left the body like a puff of air or wind. Of course no one could see this "spirit" as it was released from the lifeless body, but it seemed to be an idea that Greek people took to easily and with gusto. God wondered if Paul had heard about it, Paul who had begun preaching that Jesus had been "resurrected" and gone to Heaven to live with His Father… not only his spirit, but also his body. He remembered the morning when he held death in his arms – his mother Mary - and how her inert cooling body had felt.

God and Naomi pondered many questions, and answers were like greasy snakes.

Before they left the Greek world, Epictetus gave

them a lovely blue blanket on which they slept a few evenings outside in an olive grove. "Let us thank Zeus for this soft blanket," Naomi whispered on their last night. "And for the umbrella of stars," God added before they commenced making love. "O what a world," Naomi said as their bodies began to become one.

LXXI

For twenty years they wandered continuously to the north and east. The air got colder and for many days the sun would never rise very high in the sky. They encountered countless new faces and human forms. Eyes and hair were different. Skin was different. Clothes were thick. Animals were killed, the skins of which were used to keep the human beings warm. "People are so different, yet so similar," God said one day. "We keep walking and eventually we always find more people. No one seems to know how they got to be where they are." "Most were born quite near to where they are now," Naomi said. "I don't think many other people have walked as far or have seen as much of the world as we have." "Could the world be never ending? "I don't know."

"Why do you think we or anything else lives?" "I don't know." "It seems people have many different reasons for living." "I think most people are like animals… they don't think about 'why' they live… they just live." "And then die…" "I think I live to love you." "Why do we love?" "That I know… Without our love, life would be as empty as the space between the moon and the sun." "Do you think there is only one sun and one moon?" "It is possible, but I don't know for sure." "What do you mean?" "I mean every day we see the sun… Is it always the same sun? Or does it have brothers and sisters and they take turns visiting us? The same for the moon. It often looks different. Maybe there are many moons dancing around us…" "But we never see more than one at a time." "Yes, it makes me wonder."

They finally started moving south where they were quite sure the weather would be warmer. How did they know this? How do birds know it? They sensed they should settle down again soon and they wanted to do it in a clement climate. When they had been far to the north where for months at a time it was very cold and the sun very low, they wondered why people lived in such places. Maybe they didn't know other parts of the world were warmer. God and Naomi had tried to explain to people that there were places on the earth where the weather was very pleasant. But the people just laughed. For them there was nothing wrong with their weather. In any case, God and Naomi didn't stay long enough in these cold areas to learn the local language well. Perhaps the people simply never understood what they were trying to say.

After many years of wandering through mountains and valleys, the world started to become warmer and greener. They even began to see elephants, monkeys, strange snakes, and spiders the size of human hands. "Where do you think these creatures come from?" God asked one day. "Where does anything come from?" Naomi responded. "With every passing day the world becomes odder and odder." "I thought it would become less mysterious. But the opposite is happening." "Yes, my love."

One very warm and muggy afternoon after a torrential rain had left them wet to the bone, they were taken into a home and given food and dry clothes by a kind woman. There was no man in the house, but the woman had many children and cats. "Where are we on this earth?" they asked her gesturing with their hands and eyes. "Nan…Yang…" she said. Of course they had no idea where they were or what she meant. But they liked where they were and the woman seemed happy to have them around. They decided to stay for a while and built a little hut with palm branches next to the woman's home. They lived there for more than a decade, until all the original cats had died. But more were born. They learned the language and watched the children grow into adulthood. Some died, some had babies. The village grew.

One evening God and Naomi wandered to a river upon which a large yellow moon was shining.

"There must be more than one moon. It's not possible it can be so different from one place to another…" "I don't know." "Why does it always look bigger when it is low and near to the earth and smaller when it is high in the sky?" "How do you know when it is near or far? Maybe one moon is very big and far away and another is very small and close to the earth? Just because something is near to the eye does not make it big, even though it looks that way." "Of course." "Do you remember that white-tusked animal that we saw the other day? At first it looked small and then as we moved closer it revealed itself to be bigger than any animal we had ever seen." "There are so many things we don't know. When people say the moons are bigger than the stars I have to doubt them. When they say the heavens move, but Earth stays still, I have to doubt them. Earth? Heavens? Where is the centre?" "Why do people think there is a centre?" "Do you think we are at the centre? ... Maybe there is no centre." "I don't know.… When I take the time to think on any subject, I always begin to doubt myself. If I'm honest, the only thing I really know is that I love you." "You're such a silly beast, dear God! You sound like those monkeys that were flying through the trees and laughing at us yesterday." "They looked happy… happier than most people we meet." "What do most people have to be happy about?" "I don't know… life… and monkeys?" "What do monkeys have to be happy about?" "I wonder why the air is so different here? It is like another layer of skin, creamy and heavy, even when there are no clouds or rain falling from the sky." "Do you think the rain makes the clouds or do the clouds make the rain?" "I don't know. Sometimes there are many clouds and no rain." "Does the rain only come down from the clouds or might it go up too... in the other direction... away from the earth?" "I don't know. Only birds that fly above the clouds can know such a thing. I wonder if there are birds flying all through the heavens?" "Where do you think the heavens stop?" "Oh God, how many millions of questions can we ask? Why is it that other people don't seem to ask questions like you and I do?" "I think they are too busy living to ask such questions. Do monkeys and elephants ask questions?" "Another good question." "With no answer." "In any case, I think I like questions better than answers. Questions open doors. Answers close them." "Look how green everything is here!" "Why is there so much more rain here than in Palestine?" "I don't know... Don't you think the people here are beautiful? I love the shape of their eyes." "At first they looked strange... like everything else new... People here looked as if they were ready to sleep all the time... Now that I'm used to them, I love them... It's your oval eyes that look strange!" "These people seem to have more energy than people whose eyes stay wide open." "To them I'm sure our eyes seem as though there is something wrong with the lids." "Is it not odd how people always think their world is the 'normal' world?" "It is not odd; it is the most human of all things. We've seen it everywhere. The world always starts with oneself and one's people. Whatever is not like 'us' is always considered strange." "Have you noticed that the people here never talk about either Jehovah or Zeus?" "It is true… I've have never heard the words 'Zeus' or 'Jehovah'. They speak of different forces behind the world. I'm not sure if they're speaking of gods, but I often hear the word 'Tao'." "It seems to be the name of someone or something they care about very much. But I'm never exactly sure of the meaning of what they are saying. Languages are slippery fish." "It's interesting that everywhere we go, young children understand a language far better than we do." "Are we all born with the language of our parents in our heads?" "I don't know. We might be. Two-year-olds know little about anything, but they can talk…" "We can't remember what was happening when we were two years old, so we don't know how we learned to speak." "Remember the other evening when we tried to tell the woman what Palestine was like. I told her about the Jews, Jehovah, and how the Hebrew people believe the world was 'created'. She thought it was funny to think that the world had been 'created'." "I've been thinking about that. These people don't seem to believe that the world was made by a god. They think it has always been here." "And me… I've been thinking about my father when used to beat me and scream about 'Jehovah' and my 'sins'. Since we left Hellas the word 'Jehovah' has no meaning for anybody and I've never heard anyone talking about 'sin'." "Yes, it is a strange world, and like you said the other day, the more we see, the stranger it gets." "People here are so gentle and calm. They don't talk about having gold or wanting to get rich. They don't speak about Hell or Heaven. Here people would think my father was completely crazy for beating me. My father would think these people are all going to Hell because none of them believe in Jehovah." "They've never heard of Jehovah… Did you hear the old man yesterday in the market talking about the Tru'ang sisters?" "A little bit. They were his heroes. Sisters… women." "In Palestine all the heroes are gods or men." "Yes… He said the sisters led a rebellion against the attackers from the north that had come down to control their people. The people from the north wanted them to dress and talk like they did. But the Tru'ang sisters said "NO!" and rallied the people against the invaders." "Why would the people from the north want to impose their way of life on others?" "Because they're human…" "Did you understand the end of the story about the sisters?" "No, I don't remember. What happened?" "The people from the north trapped them in some cave or building or something. They were going to kill the sisters, but the sisters wouldn't let them because they killed themselves first." "Don't you hate the world sometimes?" "Remember what that Greek Epictetus said about not worrying about things you can't control." "Yes, it is good advice." "It seems that people here are a little less crazy than the people back home. Not all of them, but most of them." "Do want to stay here longer or shall we move on?" "If we go away, I will need some new shoes." "I will make you some. Remember, when we met I was a shoemaker." "And I was a sad child." "We've come a long way, my love." "Yes, but hasn't our voyage just begun?"

LXXII

God made the shoes. They left that part of the world and wandered for a long time through what is now China and Mongolia. They saw millions die of pestilence, hunger, cold, war, and disease. They saw thousands of mothers lose life at birth – their babies' and their own. They watched the human race struggle to survive another day, another year, another decade. When one sees so much suffering and death, there is an inevitable numbing of the mind and heart, but God and Naomi tried to feel compassion and love for every creature they encountered everywhere they went. Life was a miracle and they were part of it. But they often wondered where the limits were as to what the human spirit could endure. Was there enough joy to balance the pain? In any case, they lived on – century after century – while everyone around them perished. They saw thousands and thousands of bodies go back into the earth and many others rot away in lonely nooks and crannies, or often eaten by other forms of life.

They began to learn languages more quickly. They became fascinated by the similarities and variations from one region to the next. How old were these languages? How did they all come to be? Who made the rules? Some were written down and others were not... why? Who created the signs and symbols? One thing was certain: humans everywhere talked and humans everywhere used language to get things done and to tie each other together in one way or another.

God and Naomi were there for what history calls "the Jin dynasty". They cringed as civil wars unfolded and the vicious struggle for power sent so many young men to their graves. They heard wise old sages again talking about the "Tao", the yin and the yang, and even how the human body was a reflection of the cosmos. God asked, "Why *our* bodies, and not the bodies of birds, snakes, or sheep?" And Naomi answered, "Because man is man…"

Little by little they made a huge loop and finally headed back in the direction of the setting sun. Three hundred years had passed since they left Palestine when they arrived in the large metropolis of Constantinople. God was in for a shock: there were churches everywhere and countless representations of his father. He and Naomi had pretty much forgotten about the religion that Jesus's friend Paul had started after Jesus had died. And now, there it was, burning like a fire in the hearts of an enormous mass of people. Long-robed, thick-bearded Christian priests were everywhere all claiming to be "men of God". When God told them his name was "God" they scoffed and said calling oneself "God" was heretical. When God calmly replied that Jesus was his father and had chosen the name "God" for his only son, they all thought God was a madman and some even took pity on him. One of these "holy" men sat God and Naomi down and showed them a book, *The New Testament*, that was said to contain all the "teachings" of Jesus. God wondered where whoever wrote the book got his or her information. Mary had told God all about his father's life and little or nothing in the book corresponded to anything she had said, except that Jesus was a very kind man and that he died on a wooden cross. But the rest… the virgin mother, the miracles, the resurrection, the Kingdom of Heaven, the spirit of God, sin, angels – none of this had anything to do with what Mary had said about the love of her life.

The longer God stayed in Constantinople the more he was saddened by what the men in the long robes were saying. One day he met one such priest on the street and they had this conversation…

My dear sir, I know you don't believe me when I say I am the son of Jesus but let me tell you what my mother said about my father. You must understand that I never knew him because he died before I was born. But I knew well the woman with whom Jesus made love to make me – the woman named Mary Magdalene whom he loved to death.

Stop talking foolishness my friend.

I am not talking foolishness. You and the other priests are the ones who are talking nonsense. You know nothing about the real Jesus.

It saddens me to hear you say such a thing. But this

priest was open-minded and wanted to hear God out. *Tell me what you think you know about our Lord and Saviour Jesus Christ.*

I thank you for at least listening to me, kind sir. The other men in the long robes lend nary an ear to listen to anything I have to say.

So what kinds of things did your mother tell you?

What she told me most was that Jesus was absolutely fascinated by everything that existed. He thought life was a profound mystery.

Only God knows the truth of the world.

What god? Which god? My mother said Jesus did not know which god to believe in. He looked at the Jewish god and the Greek and Roman gods and said there was no reason to think any of them were real. That's why he wanted to name me "God"… because then he would know for sure that there was at least one real God.

God laughed when he said this, but the priest didn't.

Perhaps you are the son of Jesus, but Jesus was the Son of God.

My father never said he was the son of any divinity. He said he was the son of a man called Joseph and a woman named Mary. It was his so-called friend Paul who said Jesus was the Son of God. Jesus himself never said such a thing.

Paul was a prophet. He was a disciple of Jesus Christ. Jesus Christ is our Lord. Jesus Christ was the Son of God and He is our Saviour.

Jesus never said any of these things. It was the man Paul who made all these wild proclamations after my father had died.

They are not wild proclamations. They are the truth, the truth that is between the pages of the Holy Bible. Not only was Jesus born of the Virgin Mary, but died for the sins of the world… for my sins and your sins and the sins of all mankind.

Jesus never talked about sin. My mother told me many times that, if anything, Jesus thought men were not that different from all the other creatures that roam the earth. He said all creatures were strange, all were a mystery, and no one knew why any were what they were and acted the way they acted. My mother said Jesus never used the word "sin" to describe what men did.

But don't you know that Hell is for the world's sinners and Heaven is for those who follow the Word of God. And Jesus gave us the Word of God in the New Testament.

Jesus never spoke about a heaven or a hell. He never spoke about a god in Heaven or a devil in Hell. He only talked about this life and trying to make it as livable as possible. All he wanted to do was minimise suffering and help people to treat each other with respect and dignity.

Who was your mother?

Mary Magdalene.

Mary Magdalene was a harlot. Jesus never made love to her or to any other woman. Jesus was pure and without sin.

Why was making love to my mother a sin? They loved each other more than any man and woman have loved. God smiled and said: *At least that's what my mother told me.*

If Jesus had had a child, that child would have been born of a virgin, just like Jesus was. I am sorry to tell you that if Mary Magdalene was your mother, she was the opposite of Jesus's mother. She was a whore, a sinner and a fornicator. But how can she be your mother! She died three hundred years ago!

I should be angry with you for saying such things. But I am not the son of Jesus for nothing. Just let me say that you have no idea what you're talking about. None of you priests do. But it is not your fault. If anything, that is what Jesus – my father – taught the world. He said that stupidity is never anybody's fault. Nobody wants to be stupid. Stupidity is simply part of the world, like disease, suffering, pain, and death. You cannot help being what you are. You cannot help being so misinformed. I cannot expect you to believe that I am the son of Jesus and Mary Magdalene and that I am three hundred years old. But you should at least listen to me when I tell you that my mother loved Jesus more than any woman has ever loved a man, and Jesus loved her more than any man has ever loved a woman, and that I, God, am the fruit of their love. I am the fruit of the greatest lovemaking ever. God rubbed his belly and chest.

The priest flew into a rage and shouted… *You are deranged! You are evil! You are a blasphemer! You don't know who you are! Jesus died three hundred years ago. He was resurrected and you too will be resurrected, but you will go to Hell! … eternally damned for your blasphemy!*

God remained as calm as the morning sea…

From where do you get your idea of eternal life? From that Bible of yours? From that man Paul who told nothing but lies about my father? Yes, I am three hundred years old. But the last thing I want is to live eternally. Naomi and I just want to see as much of this world as possible. Fortunately we live longer than other people. We have seen a lot and we hope to see much more. But one day I am sure that Naomi and I will have had enough living. Then we will want to die.

The priest stepped back away from God and screamed: *The man you claim to be your father was crucified to save mankind! And you do not even want to be saved! You do not want Eternal Salvation! You do not want to be part of His sacrifice! If you are anything, you are the son of the Devil, not the son of Jesus Christ!* The priest moved towards God menacingly, his clenched teeth showing through his beard. But he did not strike him. God looked him in the eye, and then spoke in a near whisper…

My dear sir, I understand why you believe all that you believe about this life. I understand how you have been taken in by all the teachings and beliefs of your culture and civilisation. Everywhere Naomi and I have travelled we have seen the same thing. People follow the traditions of their ancestors. You have your so-called "Christian" tradition. It has spread like a fire in a forest. You have your Bible, your churches, and your long robes. But my friend, you don't have the truth. No one does. This is what my father taught. No man knows the truth about the mystery of life. My father never talked about a god. He didn't talk about life after death. He believed in this life, here and now. He believed in the earth, nothing more. We don't know where the earth begins and ends, but at least we know we walk on it. We eat and sleep and love. Some of us hate. But this earth is not some wishful eternity… some hoped-for afterlife. For Jesus, 'this life' was sacred. He claimed no knowledge about any other life or kingdom. He tried to understand people. He tried to be kind to people. He tried to make the earth as livable as possible for all people he met. That is all. God paused. The priest glared at him but said nothing. Finally God said softly, I will leave you now. My love and I are going to continue our journey, farther in the direction of the setting sun. Goodbye my friend…

LXXIII

The so-called Christian religion had, in fact, spread like a wildfire. It started in Rome and had taken hold of the hearts and minds of millions of people across that part of the world. It was squeezing human brains. It was shrinking them. It was telling them its way was the only way, that its truth was the only truth. God saw it as a disease of the mind and even the body as many of the stone-faced priests began insisting that the human body was somehow unclean, even evil, and that only the spirit counted. God knew from his mother Mary that Jesus had never separated the mind from the body, that the love of her life had appreciated the body and mind equally, and in fact, that he had never made a distinction between the two. Of this God was sure.

And now when he saw priests bellowing about how the flesh was wicked, God was saddened that his father's life was being used in such a manner. But as he and Naomi walked on, they knew it was too late. There were churches, crosses, and images of Jesus everywhere. God remembered what Epictetus said about not worrying about things you can't control. But what sorrowed them even more was that people were fighting – even killing each other – as they argued about what Jesus "really" said and taught, when, in fact, none of them had any idea what had actually come from Jesus's mouth and heart. "Jesus said that" … "Jehovah commands this" … "Do this and you will go to Heaven" … "Do that and you will burn in Hell!" – the priests exhorted the masses. It was a farce beyond measure. But Naomi and God knew there was no stopping it. Even Jesus's mother Mary got taken through the wash and had come out bleached as the whitest virgin to walk the face of the earth. Yes, God's family tree had been uprooted forever.

There was, however, one thing that some of the priests were saying that did have a few grains of truth to it: "Father forgive them for they know not what they do". Now that part of the Bible was true! Jesus had said that! And he would have forgiven those misguided priests for all the other nonsense they were spreading. Why? Because Jesus forgave everybody. Why? Because the whole universe was innocent. Everything… absolutely everything was innocent. Nothing asked to be what it was. No moon, no bug, no bee, no tree, no star, no man… not even the long-robed men with the granite faces. "The world," God said as he and Naomi walked slowly westward, "is deeper than anyone knows… far, far deeper than any human mind will ever go."

LXXIV

For the next two hundred years God and Naomi wandered through the areas now referred to as Asia Minor, the Middle East, and Northern Africa. They saw that another religion was spreading – a new fire. It – Islam – had many similarities with the Christian religion that was already rampant: there is only one God (not Jehovah, but Allah), Hell and Heaven are as real as the sun and the moon, do what the prophet says and the virgins will be waiting for you, go against the prophet's teachings and you're in for a rough life – and eternity! …Yes, two blazes were burning the minds of the people they came in contact with. Even the Greeks were talking that way.

God and Naomi just sighed… and observed. One morning when they awoke in the sand next to the creaseless sea, God said, "Naomi, I don't know what I would do without you." "I feel the same way about you God." "What a world this is! … O what a curious world." "Everywhere we go now one of these two religions is taking over people's minds." "Yes, it is as if there are no other ways to see the world, life, and the universe." "People's minds are rather simple and stale here. We must keep walking and look for new ideas and fresh air. There must be other parts of the earth where people see things differently… like where we were with the woman and her many cats and children." "Yes… but here, in this part of the world, I am beginning to wonder. I hope we can find other populations with other visions of life. It is true that many of these people are very kind, but their minds are petty and small. I know it's not their fault. But I would just as soon talk to sheep as to them." "They are sheep. Sheep with a different bleat. It is amazing how they are satisfied with such silly stories to explain the great mystery of life. It is as if they live like worms underground and never come up to see any light. Their heads are always in the thick dirt that covers the earth. And then to see them pray on their knees, their eyes closed and their noses to the ground – what a sight it is! One would think they would pray standing up with their arms raised to the sun… to light… to the open skies!" "O what a world … People are beggars satisfied with a few simple answers to the deepest questions." "But perhaps the deepest questions have no answers." "That is very possible, my love. If there is comfort in these religions, it is understandable how the gentle herds will flock to them. They will chew on whatever keeps them alive… now and forever…" Naomi took God's wrist and kissed his sun-browned arm. "Maybe that is why your parents named you 'God'… They wanted people to feel divinity every time they saw you." "The only divinity they knew was their love for each other. I was the fruit of that love. I was the God of Love." "And my parents were the opposite of yours. They knew no love of anything. They feared everything. They feared the rabbis. They feared the Romans. They feared Hell and damnation. They feared I would marry a man that was not a man of God… their god Jehovah. Little did they know that I found the one true God… my one true love." Naomi laughed and rolled on top of God.

Later they went for a swim in the sea that was melted into the azure sky.

They headed farther south. Much to their surprise and curiosity, they began to encounter humans who had skin of another different colour. Naomi and God hoped that these people's minds and ideas about life would be different as well. Their scantily clad bodies were various shades of brown and black, with little tints of purple depending on the light of the sun. They noticed that their hands and tongues were pink like those of the people up north. Many had long sleek bodies and they were a pleasant change from human beings they were used to seeing. God wondered if their blood was blackish, too, but then he remembered that his own blood wasn't the same colour as his skin and that sheep and pigs had blood very similar to his. Was rich red blood common to all living creatures? – They got their answer a few days later when they met a young woman who was in the midst of giving birth to a child. They stopped to help her and when the small black head began to poke out of the woman's womb, they saw that her blood was the same colour as theirs. And then when they encountered men with spears and knives warring with each other, again they saw thin rivers of crimson liquid leaking from the bodies of men and animals. *How does blood get into bodies?* they wondered. *Men, women, children and animals all have it and it is always the same sparkling red. Why does death occur when large quantities leak from the body? Is blood the juice of life?* … And God remembered what his mother had told him about how she was alone beneath the cross when Jesus died and how the last drops of his blood fell to her face…

On they walked, closely observing these new people. They were excited to learn their language in order to understand what they thought and how they saw the world, but they soon realized that each group they met spoke a different tongue. Interestingly, after months of walking they hadn't seen a single church or cross, nor had they heard

Jesus's name mentioned once. They were happy and relieved that the lies about God's father and mother had not spread to this part of the world. "Perhaps these people sing a different song about what existence is all about?" Naomi said one day. "Let us hope so," God said, "and let us hope that that they are happier with this world than those who speak of Allah and Jehovah and sin and fire."

After wandering for a few weeks, they were invited to settle in a place where a river ran into a large lake. They stayed for ten years – a long time for some, a puff of smoke in the imagination of others.

In general, the people were very kind. They lived simply and built fewer buildings than the humans they had known in the north. But because the air was warmer, they didn't need as much protection from the weather. What fascinated God and Naomi was that though these people were different in many ways, they still had much in common with the creatures they met throughout their travels. They wondered if there was such a thing as "the human type"? Were all men and women of the same family like all rabbits or all cats or dogs? But maybe, they thought, this way of grouping creatures was completely mistaken… Was each creature unique and to be considered as such? Or, inversely, should ALL living creatures be grouped together in ONE family of the living? … God and Naomi had no answers. But they had the questions.

One day they had this conversation:

You know, Naomi, at first I thought these people would be very different from the people of Palestine, Greece, Rome, China, Mongolia, and Vietnam. They were a different colour. Many were bigger and stronger. But in the end they are so similar. They too have explanations for where everything came from. They believe in a creator. They have a vision of right and wrong, good and bad, real and unreal. They talk about spirits and souls departing from bodies. They talk about life after death. They sometimes sacrifice animals to their divinities…

Yes, God. I have thought the same. When I look into their dark eyes I see the same hopes and fears…

Do you see these hopes and fears when you look into the eyes of a camel or a lamb?

Yes, when the lamb is ready to be slaughtered or when the camel is weary from walking.

Why do we differentiate so between men and animals?

I don't know. I have thought about this a lot. All creatures are mysteries and wonders of the world. All have eyes, hearts and blood. On what basis do we value some more than others?

It seems that human beings everywhere value certain creatures more than others. But which creatures are valued changes from place to place.

Can any man or woman say "why" they value one thing over another?

Most people value what keeps them alive. Then they value what their traditions have passed on to them. Then they value what is rare and beautiful in their eyes.

And beauty changes from one place to another.

As does the weather, the faces, the clothes, the sounds that come from mouths, what gets eaten, and the gods that are worshipped.

Can any man or woman truly explain why they do what they do? Here they chant, dance, and beat on drums in the open air. Why? In the north we saw them praying on their knees in cold churches. Why? ... why? ... why?

It seems that nobody ever looks into their own soul

and truly asks why they do what they do, why they think what they think, why they say what they say, and why they believe what they believe.

Maybe only the gods do that…

I doubt it. The gods are too busy creating universes and judging their creatures. (They laugh and kiss.)

Sometimes I think the idea of a god is the silliest idea ever to pass through a human head… Imagine thinking the universe was created… What an idea! … What a silly idea! Just because men create houses, boats, and buildings doesn't mean that everything was created. If a creator created the world, who – or what – created the creator? Such an idea always just begs the question. In any case, human beings always see the world through the eyes of human beings. Fish see the world through the eyes of fish. If there are gods, they see the world through the eyes of gods…

The deepest questions can never be answered… Never… This is what I think I have learned so far in life.

I know. I look into the bottom of my heart to try to understand why I love what I love. I have asked myself a thousand times why I love you and only you. And of course I can never explain it. If I can't explain what is closest and dearest to me, how can I expect to explain something outside of myself?

You can't… we can't.

And how can anyone expect to explain someone else's behaviour? Or an animal's behaviour?

Here, in this part of the world, I am so amused at how the shamans tell people what is causing what and what people should and shouldn't do. And the people are satisfied. People everywhere are satisfied with answers from those who are supposed to know. In the north it was the priests. When we were children it was the rabbis with their Bibles and Romans with their whips.

I believe no one. Everywhere we go I see the blind following the blind.

Everywhere we go there are people who are supposed to know more than others… people who are supposed to have the secrets to life's questions and dilemmas. It is fascinating how their followers believe them.

It is the human way. It is what we see everywhere… some have the power and others bow down to it. Some claim to have knowledge and the others acquiesce to it.

It is interesting how sometimes the powerful are gentler in some places than in others.

Here they have taken us in with open arms. They were not afraid of us.

They have been kind. Saying goodbye will not be easy.

Can you imagine the day we say goodbye to life.

I have tried many times to imagine it. I think that as I breathe my last breath I will whisper, "What was that…?"

Yes, life is such a mystery.

The only thing I know is that I want to breathe my last breath with you, my darling. Love is when life does not make sense without the other.

Does it ever make sense?

Only in the life of love…

After ten years, God and Naomi said goodbye to their dark-skinned friends and headed back up north. When they met pale faces again they seemed very odd, as did their smaller noses and lips, and the straight hair that dropped down on their shoulders. But little by little, their minds and eyes adjusted. Soon the Caucasian type looked normal again.

LXXVI

As they wandered, they wondered how much more world there was to see. One morning, after many years of walking in the direction of the setting sun, they came upon a vast beach. They stood and stared at the incessant waves. The water continuously flowed towards them, lapping the shore, then disappearing back into the motherly sea. They had a bit of food and water, so they sat and ate. Their eyes saw only sand, water, a long flat line, and blue sky. There was nothing else… absolutely nothing else.

What could be out there? Naomi asked. *Could there be more land? Could there be more creatures similar to those we have seen?*

I don't know. If there are more creatures, I think I

would be more interested in their minds than their bodies. We have seen many fascinating people and animals. Sometimes the animals are more fascinating than the people... They both thought of the lions, giraffes, hippos, rhinos, monkeys, birds, cheetahs, antelopes, and gorillas that they had seen living near their dark-skinned friends... *There might be more amazing creatures somewhere. But what I'd like to see are some amazing minds... minds that turn the world inside out... minds that have not been put to sleep by the traditions around them, minds that do not see the world around them as normal and commonplace, but who see mystery, tragedy, beauty, and infinity... in everything! It is sad how so many human beings are so lacking in curiosity and wonder. Many, if not most, are no more curious than the cows that were eating grass all day in the fields we have just crossed.*

I don't know if it is sad. Is being a cow a sad thing? Perhaps simplicity is a good thing for most creatures. Too much complexity might be bad for them, just like it might be bad for many human minds.

You might be right, my love. I don't know why I always expect humans to be something other than what they are. It is a silly prejudice I have. I don't do it for monkeys and sheep and cows... so why should I do it for people?

You just always hope people will be better. You want the best for everybody and every creature, from the largest to the smallest. You are not Jesus's son for nothing.

And you are not my love for nothing... You know Naomi, human beings might be some of the best creatures, but they are also some of the worst. They are the only creatures that kill for a god they have never seen or heard speak. They seem to be the only creatures that kill without wanting to eat what they kill. They can kill for land and power and leave the dead lying on the field of battle. Is anything more barbaric than that? I can't help wanting them to be less cruel and stupid. You never see a butterfly or a sheep causing harm to another creature. Few animals are cruel. They are usually only cruel when they are trying to protect themselves. Man can be cruel for many other reasons. It is that that I hope will change.

But it is very possible that man will never change.

Yes, it is... Why should he change? What part of him might make him change? Don't most men think that how they live and how they think makes perfect sense... to them?

They were silent for a long while. The sun

dropped towards the empty horizon. They watched it disappear and marvelled again at the colours that appeared in the sky – stripes of red, orange, yellow, violet, and blue. Then slowly the water and sky darkened and stars filled the black above them. They lay down on the blanket on the sand. When God said, *I want to find a way to go out on the water and see what is there,* Naomi didn't hear him. She was already asleep. Her lovely legs and mind had walked many miles that day.

LXXVII

For years and years they wandered up and down the coast, but they met no one who had found a way to explore the vast sea stretching endlessly towards the setting sun. People seemed to fear what was out there, fear how far it went, and fear that anyone who ventured forth would eventually fall off and drop into the depths of space. God was not so sure. He once held an apple in his hand and ran his finger around its smooth skin. It came back to the place it had started. From that moment onward he wondered if the world might be shaped like the apple. Was the sun flat? Was the moon flat? The apple wasn't flat? Perhaps Sun, Moon, and Earth were as round as apples!

Of course God was not the only one who had

had this thought. But such thinkers were few and God and Naomi had rarely met such a person.

In the meantime, God and Naomi had begun hearing rumours that in the other direction – in the direction of the rising sun – people were massacring each other in great numbers in Jesus's name. God was deeply saddened and wondered anew how man could be such a cruel beastly creature.

Really, Naomi, why do you think they do such things? God asked one morning as they walked in the sand under a warming sun.

The same answer always comes into my mind… Why does any creature behave the way it does at any moment? Who can say? Who can understand? Who can know? Sometimes I think that any question beginning with "why" is a ridiculous one? Why is the sky blue? Why is this beach here and not over there? Why water here and not there? Why do we ask our questions? Why do people everywhere invent gods? Why do we even think? Why do we feel joy and pain? Why do people kill each other in the name of their divinities? Every answer just begs another question. In the end there are no answers. Both the questions and answers can go on forever. There is no solace when one takes the mind in such a direction.

Yes, my darling, and that is why I look to love for solace. It is the only place where my mind stops and is at peace. Otherwise it just keeps digging deeper and the hole keeps getting bigger.

I know, dear God, but we too are human and we too have minds and bodies that we can't always control.

They were alone. They removed their clothes and made love in the sand.

What they had heard about the people slaughtering each other was not just rumour. The so-called Christians were killing the Jews and Muslims who did not agree with their view of life and the world. The stone-faced men in the long robes were sending out armies in the name of God to cleanse the earth of the so-called "infidels". *They're all infidels,* God thought. *They abuse my father's life and worst of all, they abuse life on this earth. They are all worms with theirs heads in the ground.*

Fortunately the day God had been waiting for came. One morning as he and Naomi were strolling near the sea, they saw a throng of men building an enormous boat. They approached the site and questioned the man who was shouting orders and seemed the leader…

What are you planning to do with this beautiful vessel?

We want to see if there is an end to the ocean. We want to see if there are other lands and people out there. Some men are saying the earth is round like an orange and that if we keep going we can come back to where we started.

What do you *think, my good man?*

The man looked at God's gentle face and wondered if he had ever seen such eyes of empathy and compassion. *I don't know,* he said. *But I want to find out.*

I share your questions and your ideas, God said. *I once held an apple and thought maybe the earth was shaped like fruit. You think it might be like an orange.*

In any case, it is a mystery and I want to find the answer to this and many other questions.

You are brave to want to venture into the unknown. I doubt there are many men so brave as you. God watched the man's head turn as he looked toward the open sea.

One day we will find out what is out there, he said

pointing to the ocean. *And then another day we will find out what is out "there".* And his arm and finger shot up towards the sky.

I don't think I've ever met a man like you, God said. He looked at Naomi and she seemed to concur. Then he looked carefully at the man and without more ado said, *Sir, can Naomi and I join you? We have walked for many many years and have seen much of the world. We too have wondered if there is more... if there is more world, different creatures, new places, new people, and new minds. Dear sir, we could work on your ship. We could help prepare the food for you and your men. We could help with the cleaning and the washing of your raiment.*

The man looked at God and Naomi, their tattered clothes, and their serene faces. *But who are you?* he asked. *Where do you come from? How long have you been walking?*

I am God and this is Naomi. We come from afar where once the Jews and Romans cohabitated. But we left a very long time ago. We have been walking the earth for hundreds of years...

The man wondered if he was talking to a chimera. He had never heard such a voice of peace and serenity. *Do you know anything about boats and sailing the sea?*

We have little experience with water, but we have much experience with life. We have been on the earth for about fifteen hundred years.

The man's face lit up with a smile. He wondered if God and Naomi were mad or simpletons. But for some reason he was touched and his curiosity was piqued.

So, my good fellow, why did you call yourself "God"?

Because that is the name my father and mother gave me.

And who are your father and mother?

Jesus Christ and Mary Magdalene, the most wonderful mother and father a man has ever had.

The man began laughing and he gently tapped God on the shoulder. But he could not refuse such kindness. He even imagined that he might need such people on the boat… imaginative people, perhaps slightly crazy, but people with no fear and nothing to lose, people who might amuse him and the other sailors. He thought for a moment and said, *Yes, my friends, you can come with us. We plan to leave in one month's time. So come back after thirty suns have risen and fallen. I will have a place for you on the boat.*

We will be here, kind sir. We are as grateful for you as we are for life…

The ship's captain watched them turn and walk away arm in arm.

LXXVIII

During the next four weeks God and Naomi often wondered if they would ever return to their known world again. And they thought more and more about death. Though any thinking person knows death is possible every minute of every day, we can go long stretches of our lives without a thought of dying. Then suddenly, for whatever reason, death can become an obsession. What is it? Is it definitive? Might death just be another phase of life? Though God and Naomi had lived for nearly fifteen centuries – longer than any other human or animal on Earth – they too had periods when they thought little about the subject. But as the days clicked away towards their departure, they felt death like burnt skin…

Naomi, we soon might never see any of this again.

Yes, God. Not only might we never see any of this again, we soon might not see any of anything again.

Ah, dying, my love, is the greatest mystery of all...

Haven't you often said that there are two great mysteries: death and love.

I have often said that everything is a mystery (God chuckled as if he had just retold a worn-out joke and waved his arms at the sky). *But yes... you are right... For me death and love are two of the subjects that have kept my mind spinning the most.*

Is that what minds do... spin?

I have no idea. Can you think of a better word?

Trot?... gallop?... waltz?... wander?... fly like birds?... slither like snakes?... buzz like bees?... My dear God, I have no idea how a mind works, what pushes it on, what happens when death strikes... It too is a great mystery.

That is one reason why I've always thought dying will be interesting... We'll finally get to see if the mind lives on in some form or another.

Or we won't get to see that...

Yes, my love... Anyway, there are enough mysteries in life to keep even the vainest man humble and the most intelligent man in a state of wonder...

Let's hope this boat will take us to a new world, where we can live and love a little bit more...

In any case, before they left they tried to taste, feel, see, and touch as much of their known world as they could. They sucked the juice from oranges and lemons. They stared at flowers and examined their petals. They climbed hills and visited castles. They caressed cats, sheep, goats, and dogs. They watched birds and butterflies glide and bounce through the air. They sipped wine and ate tomatoes, cheeses, aubergines, potatoes, bread, and olives. Whenever God put an olive in his mouth he thought of his mother.

Naomi, do you remember my mother?

I only saw her for one day, but she left me a memory for a thousand years.

And to think she died that night we slept together for the first time... in her bed. It is a beautiful thought: she died in my bed while we were making love in hers.

You were so lucky to have had such a mother. I'm glad I saw her, even for only a day.

Yes... The other day I was thinking... I have observed myself for so many years I have come to an evident conclusion: I am happiest when two conditions are present… First, when my state of mind is that it is impossible to make sense of the world, that the world – and all existence – is so great a mystery, that it is ridiculous to think that one can understand why one thinks what one does, that we can never understand what causes what because everything goes back too far, and at the same time being so grateful that anything exists at all… And the second condition is that I must be with the woman I truly love… Before it was my mother and now it is you… God's eyes filled with tears of joy.

Naomi covered God's face with kisses. *And I feel much the same thing…*

They were both quiet for a long moment and for whatever reason, God said, *I wonder why the Jews and Christians think the world needs to be redeemed? … Redeemed from what? I would say the only redeemer in this world is love… true love… love like ours… and Jesus and Mary's. Only love can pull us above the tragedy of the human condition… not just the human condition… but the condition of all creatures… and all things… all things that are stuck in the quicksand of existence… I've said it many times before and I'll say it again… Nothing can be other than what it is… And love is the only way of breaking free. In love one's being is mixed with another's. In love one becomes two and two become one. That is the only freedom I know.*

And when I think that my parents never found real love on this earth, it greatly saddens me.

There is much to be sad about, my love... but there is as much to cause us to rejoice.

I would not have known it had I not met you, God.

Naomi's and God's eyes met through a double veil of tears. One can only cry so much in this world. There is a limit to the amount of pain and sadness one can feel. And there is only so much joy one can have before the mind and body explode. Tears of tragedy are best shed alone. Tears of love must be shared.

LXXIX

The four weeks had nearly passed. Soon the great ship would be leaving. God and Naomi decided to write a letter… a letter to "Life". They used a mixture of languages that they had picked up over the centuries. Translated, it went like this:

Dear Life,

In a few days we will be venturing into the unknown with about thirty other men. We will head in the direction of the setting sun, into the vast empty sea, hoping to find out how big our world is, if it is round or flat, and if there are other kinds of living things upon it. We have seen much; we hope to find more. We are well aware that we may never return to "this" world. We may be sucked into the ocean. We may disappear. We may die and drift into the other great unknown...

Before we go, we just want to thank you – life – for existing. You are the miracle of miracles, the greatest wonder of all. Every day we rejoice at the fact that there is something and not nothing.

As we may not come back, we would like to leave a few thoughts for all the human beings on this earth, all you creatures that share the blessing – and sometimes the curse – of language:

First, friends, when all is said and done, you should admit, once and for all, that you have no idea who and what you are. You think you know, but you don't. We have observed that most of you think you were created by some grand all-powerful God, and this thought gives your life value and meaning. But we want to tell you it is very possible that there is no such a Being. The only real God we have encountered in our fifteen hundred years on Earth is a man named God, a man of flesh, blood, and bones like all of you – a man who may die soon. Most of you think Jesus was the Son of God. But no, this man was the son of Jesus Christ and Mary Magdalene and they named him "God". Jesus's parents were human and my parents were human… as human as these thirty brave men with whom we are going into the unknown. God never knew his father Jesus. He died an absurd death on a wooden cross months before God was born. But God lived with his mother Mary for eighteen years. She told him many times that she and Jesus gave him the name God such that the world would be sure to have at least one real god.

So, let us ask this question: if we, the people of this earth, are not the children of a divine god, then what are we? Do we have any idea? We think we do not. We are convinced that all existence is a great mystery. No one knows where the world came from. No one knows how anything got here. We have walked far and wide, certainly farther and wider than any other people. We have seen people of all kinds. We have listened, observed, and walked beside millions. And we have found that essentially nobody asks one crucial question… "And what if there is no God? What then? What are we… really?" Yes, what are we really? And if we are honest, we have no idea. We have our traditions and our various prophets and wise men. We tend to be satisfied with their answers. But after what we have observed all over the known world, we fear that all our explanations are mistaken. Let us be clear, there is nothing wrong with being mistaken because these answers give people comfort and meaning. But, we ask, wouldn't it be a wonderful day – a day of great liberation – if just once we all climbed out of our caves of delusions and untruths and looked straight into the light of existence, raised our arms toward the infinite, and declared…"Dear universe, you are such a mystery… the grandest mystery of all!"?

If and when someone finds this message, perhaps people will finally have stopped believing in the Christian God, the Islamic God, the Jewish God, and all the other gods. And when they do, they will stop saying that God created the universe and mankind. But we fear they will replace one explanation with another. We know that man's need for answers is so strong and we are afraid he will simply come up with a new idea about the origin of life. Perhaps he will start saying that he is the summit of some great process… some grand "becoming"… that has left man on top of the totem pole. He will then declare himself to be the highest creature. And then he will say that he and only he can know the truth about where he came from. He will continue to subtly look down on other creatures and will see the rest of nature as somehow inferior to himself… somehow of lesser value and importance. And in a sense he will be right, for man is superior to other creatures in his ability to do certain things. But he forgets that other creatures can do things he can't. No man can fly like an eagle. No man can smell like a dog. No man can jump like a cat. Yes, man excels in his ability to build objects like shoes and ships, but he is also the king of killing. He is far superior to other creatures in his ability to destroy life. He is perhaps the most powerful creature, but that does not make him the best creature. If anything, it makes him perhaps the most immoral creature. By seeing himself to be outside of nature – above nature – he pretends he wears a moral crown. But we fear he will never know what good and evil are because he does not know what reality is…

But we believe that a great day will come. We don't know when, but we think that finally man will realise – and openly admit – that he has absolutely no idea who and what he is – or, for that matter, what anything else is. He will stand in awe at the absolute mystery of Being. We believe this will be the greatest moment on Earth, the moment when man finally becomes truly humble and is finally able to see himself in the mirror of reality. It will be the moment when man is truly "good", the moment when mankind begins to respect all existence, the moment from which mankind can move forward past its silly visions of history wherein it puts itself at the centre of things.

Friends, we believe there is no centre. We believe existence didn't come from anywhere, was not created by anyone, does not have a goal nor a reason or logic. Existence simply is. And it is beautiful and amazing… Perhaps you who are reading this have come to agree with us. We are sure you will be wonderful people.

So now, as we prepare to sail away with the captain and his brave men, we want to again thank you Life for being there. We want to tell you that we accept your inscrutability, we accept the fact that every moment of existence is shrouded in mystery.

And we thank you for the other great mystery – love – which, in our case, has kept us from going crazy in this stupendous world.

Now, as we finish this letter, we hear your deep silence. Ah! you are in us and we are in you, somehow together… Forever?
Love,
God and Naomi

They put the letter in an old clay pot and buried it in an olive grove near the Spanish port of Palos.

The next day God and Naomi went to the port where the majestic boat was sitting on the water like a floating mountain. All was bustle. Captain Colon was shouting orders and his men were scurrying about like ants. Naomi and God were told to help the group of eight men who were loading the food in the hull. Given that they had no idea how long they would be at sea and whether or not they would find food out there, they packed as much as they could. Colon, like God, thought there was a very good chance that the world was shaped like an apple and that it was possible for them to get to the other side of the world – to some of the places God and Naomi had visited – by going west instead of east. But nobody was sure and nobody knew how far they might have to go or how long it might take.

(We tend to forget how long the world existed before humans went all the way around it. What was the age of the earth – and mankind – when Magellan finally made the full circle? Ask a human being and he or she will give you a number. Ask the universe and it will give you a wink and a smile.)

The next morning they said goodbye to the world they knew. Other than the captain and God and Naomi, most of the crew members were criminals who had been given the choice between prison or a voyage into the unknown. The trip could have been quite a problem for Naomi given that she was the only woman on board. In spite of her one thousand five hundred years of living, she still had the charm of an unwithered rose. Captain Colon, understanding the potential explosiveness of the situation, informed the crew that immediate death would be the punishment for any man that laid a finger on Naomi. Hence, she and God were able to travel in relative peace. In fact, as they were responsible for the preparation and distribution of food, everyone wanted to stay on their good side.

As the days passed Naomi and God were awestruck by the humanity and bestiality of the crew. They saw incredible courage, strength, and comprehension as they watched the men fight together against high winds and treacherous seas. And then, when there was little wind and nothing to do, they saw despair, fear, sometimes weakness and jealousy. They saw some of the roughest men become peacemakers when fights broke out on board. When the fights were finished, the loser would often cower like a frightened mouse in a corner of the deck while the victor stared at the emptiness before them with the eyes of a sphinx.

One thing was certain: Captain Colon was an almighty leader and nobody seemed interested in taking his place.

After five weeks of generally favourable winds, they spotted land. They did not cheer or gloat as we might think, but rather stood next to the railing and gazed ahead with frozen eyes. What would they find? Should they prepare for war or peace? Had they made it around the world to India? At least there was firm land and it was getting nearer by the second.

There were people on the sand. Human beings

much like themselves – excepting their clothes, skin tint, and hair flow – were waiting for them. Colon told everyone to be on their guard, but to be as calm as possible… and to do nothing until he gave the order.

The people on the beach waved them ashore. Colon and four other men got in a small boat and went to greet them. Colon and the local chief talked, but naturally neither said anything that made any sense to the other. But all was peaceful, and with sign language it became clear that Colon and his group were welcome to anchor the boat and come on land. One of history's most incredible moments passed with astonishing ease and fluidity. What happened in the decade that followed was an entirely different story.

God and Naomi had enjoyed the experience on the boat and had deeply appreciated the crew's hospitality, but they didn't want to continue with them. They yearned to immediately go off on their own and explore this new land. The day after their arrival, they thanked Colon and hugged each of the men. Then off they went again, hand in hand, into the "New World".

They quickly saw that it really wasn't new at all. It was simply a bit different. The people had arms and legs, heads and hair, noses and mouths, fingers and toes, age and youth, and language. What struck them most was the calm and kindness of these new humans. Rarely had they been greeted and treated so warmly.

After a few months of wandering, they realised they were on a rather large island, but an island nonetheless. Was this island the end of land and people? Was there more out there? As soon as they were able to understand the language, they were told that there was "more… much more", and fingers were pointed in various directions. More land was evidently not too far to the north, west, and even the south.

God and Naomi were happy to see that these people seemed to say nothing about the god Jehovah, Jesus, the Virgin Mary, or any of the prophets and commandments in the Bible. None of that meant anything to them. They did however, seem to have a slew of other gods and explanations, which of course came as no surprise to God and Naomi. Once they watched strong men and leaders get into two small boats and head off to sea. Within a few days they were back with hulls full of fruits bursting with colour and flavour that they had never seen before.

God and Naomi were happy with these people until, a few years later, Captain Colon returned to the island with more sailors, soldiers, and a group of so-called "missionaries". God and Naomi were astounded to see that suddenly the Christian religion was being forced into the heads of these people. They were merciless; if the local people did not accept what the missionaries told them, they were threatened or killed. Many were taken into slavery and forced to look for gold or to build things for the newcomers. They saw men being forced into the boats and taken back across the ocean. What had been a placid world was being turned into torment and appalling violence. God and Naomi could not believe their eyes and were abhorred by what they saw, even though they had seen such horror and gore before in other parts of the world. But here, in this tropical paradise of sorts, it was shocking to behold. They tried to reason with the soldiers and missionaries by explaining that these people were kind and good and perfectly entitled to a different way of life. But it did no good. The invaders (and invaders they were) were sure of their god and they wanted gold. Most of them had no respect for the lifestyle of the native people. God and Naomi cringed as they observed the spectacle of human dogmatism, intolerance, greed, and flat-headedness. They could do nothing to prevent it and wanted to get off the island as quickly as possible. They were finally able to gain passage on a boat whose captain assured them that they would be transported to different *terra firma* within two or three days.

He had told the truth. As soon as they were close to land they thanked the captain, jumped off the ship and swam to the shore. There was not a soul in sight. After drying off on a lovely golden beach, they wandered inland meeting only animals – alligators, bats, monkeys, opossums, mongooses, huge butterflies, moths, and snakes. They thought that perhaps this land was devoid of people... a new Garden of Eden, and they (they jokingly said) were Adam and Eve. For a few months they lived with the animals and survived on pineapples and, of course, their love.

They kept moving. Were there other people? They

didn't count the days or nights, but eventually, they encountered a group of human beings. They looked much like the people Naomi and God had lived with on the island, though their language was quite different. They, too, were very kind and lived a simple existence. Their houses had no real walls, but were platforms attached to poles under ceilings of palm branches. They slept above the ground and out of the reach of crawling creatures.

Naomi and God decided not to stay, but to keep exploring. Slowly but surely they met many different groups, but rarely did they stay long enough to learn the local language. Often they would walk for many weeks alone. All the people they encountered tended to be calm and seemed satisfied with their lot in life. None seemed bent on belligerence. Like the islanders before the arrival of the missionaries, it was obvious that none of these societies had any notion whatsoever of the Christian God, and there was no parading of God's father Jesus agonising on the cross. Understanding what they could, they remarked that nobody ever seemed to talk about guilt, sin, Heaven or Hell. God imagined that his father would have appreciated these people. Many groups used the words "Wakan

Tanka" to talk about their feelings about life. From what they could garner, it meant something like "The Great Mystery". These human beings also seemed to respect animals as much as people. In some ways they it seemed that they saw animals to be superior to people given that they could do things people couldn't do like fly and glide above the world, or run and jump much faster and higher than men. In fact, it eventually became clear that some of their gods were beautiful creatures from their jungles and forests.

One night as Naomi and God were falling asleep, they had this conversation:

How much longer do you want to keep walking?

I don't know. But I am enjoying these people. However, I fear for them. I can feel the winds of change.

Which winds do you mean? Some winds are pleasant and cooling, whereas others are fierce and knock down trees and destroy villages.

The latter, my love. I fear that the missionaries — and others from across the sea — will come here in large numbers and little by little they will destroy these people.

You mean like what we saw before on that first island?

Yes. I can feel the land beneath our feet will one day be completely different. This part of the world will look like that other part of the world. We have seen it everywhere. The powerful eat the weak. And they always take control in the name of their god. We have witnessed it over and over.

But these people here do not seem to want to take over the weak. They appear satisfied with what they have. They don't speak of gold and riches and conquering.

And that is precisely why I fear they will disappear – because their vision of life is not one of superiority and conquest. They respect animals as much as each other. They respect the sun, the moon, the earth, the trees, the fish, the alligators, and even the snakes that flee at the sound of their feet. They do not want to dominate other creatures. They want to live with them. Colon and his people want gold, mammon, and aggrandisement. They see other creatures only in terms of what they can do to help them enrich themselves.

You know God, in general I prefer these people to the ones on the other side of the great ocean. Their eyes seem to be open wider. Their hearts are bigger. Their heads hold less hatred.

And from what we have seen so far, they do not massacre in the name of God. They do not conquer in the name of God. They do not threaten in the name of any god… We saw on the other side of the sea how the people build more, expand more, and simply seem to want more, including a trip to Heaven after they die. These people want less. They are more satisfied with what they have. Their needs are minimal. But this will be their downfall. They will perish when Christian fervour disembarks in greater numbers and with greater guns and weaponry. One needn't be visionary to see this.

Naomi and God talked no more that night. Time stopped. The world froze. They fell asleep in each other's arms.

LXXXI

One might ask how God and Naomi were able to travel so long together and not "explode" as a couple. (Even my dear conservative mother said that a couple should "travel" together before getting married as it was the only real way to see if people were truly compatible. God and Naomi took her advice to heart.) Didn't they fight? Didn't they get on each other's nerves? Didn't they get tired of each other's company after fifteen centuries together? … No, they didn't, for the simple reason they had really become one person. Their minds and bodies had woven together such that neither felt whole without the other. Once they realised this, there was no longer the question of whether or not they loved each other, because they were love. They had fused into one mind, one body, one love, much like two streams come together at the foot of the mountain to make a lake or a pond. This happens very rarely on Earth with human beings. But like a mother and a baby inextricably linked in the womb, so God and Naomi were one. The cosmos was their womb. Naomi's mind was inside God's mind; God's mind was inside hers. Their beings had fused… But let us be clear: We are not arguing that this is necessarily a good thing. Perhaps, for some, it is better to be a lone wolf in the forest. Perhaps sometimes solitude is preferable to love. But in the case of Naomi and God, real love had become a reality. If clouds, water, and atoms can fuse, there is no reason why people can't. Without the fusion of hydrogen and oxygen, there would be no life on Earth. Without the fusion of God and Naomi this story would never have been told.

Of course, in the beginning, like all couples, they had had their little moments of fear and jealousy. When you love like they loved each other, you tend to think that the whole world loves the other person the way you do. When you are apart, you think every member of the opposite sex will fall in love with your paramour just like you did. You see everyone as a potential enemy who might steal your beloved. You are enveloped by fear. You tremble like Kierkegaard who thought no human relation could ever be trusted, could ever be permanent, stable, fixed. For Kierkegaard, only a relation with God could be solid and forever… Well, that's what happened – Naomi had her God, Kierkegaard had his. They were different Gods, of course, but the result was the same: true love lasting for as long as eternity does.

God and Naomi came to realise quite early that all the problems they had between each other simply came from – and because of – their deep and abiding love. Every negative feeling or emotion for the other (the jealousy, the fear of loss) was because of their love. They came to understand that it was silly to bicker about things that might threaten their love, but which, in the end, only confirmed it. Once they understood – like the great sage Winnie-the-Pooh – that "it all comes from loving honey so much", God and Naomi's union was never menaced again.

LXXXII

After decades of watching the conquest and annihilation of the area that is today called Central America, Naomi and God had had enough. They hoped for one thing: that they would never witness such horror on such a massive scale again. But there was much more to come.

Fortunately, as is seemingly always the case on Earth, they did not only witness cruelty, greed, destruction, suffering, and slaughter, but they also saw many acts of kindness, tenderness, and goodness of heart. The world is never all bleakness. There are always acts of understanding, compassion, contemplation, and warmth on all sides. God and Naomi were spectators to some of the worst atrocities ever to befall the human race, but they also saw sharing, sacrifice, creation, hope, love, and joy. The world always has many faces. Sometimes they wondered if there wasn't, in fact, a strange hidden balance of things? Is there a kind of equilibrium to what goes on in life? For every act of cruelty is there an act of kindness? Somehow the world continues to function. Is existence a stream of opposites struggling and pushing each other onward? Is life a dialectic of some kind? Is one man's success always another man's failure? Do joy and pain exist in equal proportions? Are the scales balanced when it comes to loving and hating? Then again perhaps these terms were all human inventions which, in the end, had nothing to do with anything real – nothing to do with the blood and guts of life. They asked themselves, "What is a civilisation? When does such a thing start? When does it end? Does it start when the first person dreams or sets up his or her tent? Does it end when the last person dies? Perhaps Egypt never really started and never really disappeared. And Rome? It's still there. It's still on the map… centuries and centuries after it 'fell'… Human beings love to lay out the pieces of the puzzle on a big flat table and then put them together to make a neat clean whole picture. They love to make sense of things. But God and Naomi had come to see that the world is not a puzzle that can be broken into bits and pieces. It is one continuous flow – one great river, one enormous ocean of life and death, coming and going, appearing and disappearing. Jesus had flowed into the Jews and the Romans and the man Paul. The Christian river flowed into Islam which flowed into the Dark Ages and Middle Ages. Mr. Colon built his boats and sailed west, and then… and then… and then… The world does not stop. It is an eternal flow of water, land, flesh, blood, and brain. Nothing is pure. There are no pure people, pure thoughts, pure principles, or pure races. Time cannot be cut up. Events cannot be separated. The ocean of humanity is no different from the ocean of the world. There is no dividing line between the oceans. It is all one body of water. All is linked. People who try to break history into pieces and weave their tapestries of truth and hang them on the walls of the great halls of knowledge are all mistaken. None has the true picture.

God and Naomi walked and wondered. Of all the humans they had observed in the world, which group was the most open to life, to others, to feeling and understanding, to man's proper place in the world? But did man have a proper place? Were the people who were destroyed by the missionaries in their proper place? Didn't the invaders think that they were in their proper place? Would they be gone too one day? Don't all civilisations eventually disappear only to be misunderstood and falsely judged by posterity?

For two years they walked south on an isthmus that would take them to another huge continent where another great civilisation was prospering, only to soon be partially annihilated. They knew it was only a matter of time until enough boats crossed the ocean from the east – boats loaded with guns, Bibles, and diseases. And that time had already arrived. The soldiers and missionaries were already climbing ashore. These native inhabitants too would soon see much of their world shattered. Power is like a tsunami whose only justification is itself. But men like to mix morality with power. The formula is simple: call yourself "good" and what you conquer, "evil" and "inferior".

One spring day they sat down near a river to drink and rest. A crocodile swam by. Then another.

Neither was hungry and God and Naomi were not bothered or frightened. They stretched out on the ground and soon were sleeping. They were awakened by an enormous snake that was crawling over their warm bodies. They remained still and let it slither. It let them be. It had just finished digesting a small monkey and God and Naomi were of no more interest than a rock or a tree. When it was gone Naomi said, "I used to be afraid of snakes." "We have seen many. Now we know what to expect." "In general, if you leave them alone, they do the same to you." "So it is with most people." "I often try to imagine what goes on in the mind of a snake. How does it think? What is real for it? How does it perceive us? If no words go through its head, how does it make sense of us… and the world?" "I don't know. Perhaps it is too intelligent for words and concepts and has no use for them. It might be that it apprehends existence in a way we can't." "Do we understand how 'we' apprehend?" "Sometimes I think we, too, just slide and glide through life... over land and over people... never really knowing or understanding what we touch." "Yesterday I was petting a cat and I wondered what the connection between the two of us really was.

How closely could we feel each other?" "It would seem that we never know."

They stayed on the riverbank until the world darkened and the moon appeared. "Do you think the moon is moving? Maybe we are moving? It would make just as much sense to say that the earth is moving as to say the moon is moving." "Perhaps both are moving, like two people crossing each other on a path." "Might the path not be moving, too?" "If what we are standing on is moving, maybe what is under what we are standing on is moving, too." "And what if everything is moving all the time?" "Will we ever know?" "And I wonder about all the parts that are moving in my head and body… the ones that make me see, hear, feel, think, talk, walk, and desire to be with you." "It's all part of the mystery." "The mystery that so few seem to feel…" "Do you think the snake that crawled across our bodies feels it?" "What?" "The mystery." "I don't know, but I doubt it. If there is one thing that separates creatures, it is the ability to sense the unknown." "Yes. That… and the capacity to love." "Don't you think greatest lovers feel the greatest mystery?" "Yes, those who feel the greatest mystery are capable of the greatest love." "Can we be sure?"

"No." "What are you sure of?" "Love and mystery. The rest slips away like water on the skin of a snake."

LXXXIII

They walked along the coast as far south as they could. Then they turned back northward. A hundred years passed. Two hundred. Much of the original population had been either killed or conquered. The people were mixing, but the light-skinned men had the power. They could be seen everywhere toting guns and telling people what to do. The autochthons were doing the hard labour, cutting trees, building houses, cultivating fields, and carrying the loads.

Naomi and God watched this flow of humanity. They flowed with it. They tried to imagine the life of every person they came in contact with. They knew there were limits to compassion. You can only care so much. You can only understand so much.

The local people were being replaced by new "local" people. Perhaps thousands of years before the same process had gone on. Now, after a couple of hundred years, the Spanish and Portuguese missionaries and slave-traders were becoming indigenous. In any case, God's fears had become reality. The invaders had spread north, south, and west like blood oozing from a wound. The Lord God and His Son Jesus were constantly invoked, prayed to, feared, thanked, and worshipped.

The human God was walking with Naomi. As they got farther north they suddenly began to hear two new languages: the French and English had arrived. These speakers too had come across the ocean. Their hair tended to be a bit lighter than the Portuguese and Spanish. But they too carried the guns and swords.

LXXXIV

The years wore on. Nations were being formed. Constitutions were written. The people with the light skins were demanding independence from the kings and queens back on the other side of the ocean who were taxing them and demanding that they send back goods. Thousands of new slaves with deep purple-black skins were arriving in boats from afar. After almost eighteen hundred years of walking, God and Naomi arrived in a place that called itself "The United States of America". It was bustling, as masses of people were arriving from Europe trying to find what they called a better life. Who could argue with a creature that wanted to improve its lot? Of course few of these people thought about or understood how their better life meant a worse life for the native people. But man has never been very insightful when it comes to seeing the other side of things.

Slowly but surely this new country was split and a vicious internal war broke out. For once, the newcomers were not killing the indigenous people, but had taken to slaughtering each other. Naomi and God watched in horror as young men were thrown into the battle, maiming each other with bullets and bayonets. Again they observed how both sides swore that they had divine powers behind them and in their underpants. Blood and soiled sweat watered the earth for four gruesome years until finally the Southern side waved a white flag. The mess was cleaned up, the dead never came back, the charcoal-skinned slaves could no longer be owned. Soon after, the remaining so-called Indians were herded onto – into – "reservations". Yes, the slaves had been unchained, but that did not necessarily mean their lives were quickly made better. And the so-called Indian reservations got smaller and smaller when the white men found gold on them and, in the end, were usually located on the land the government and pioneers wanted the least.

But the powerful new nation continued to grow and expand to the west. God and Naomi wandered everywhere. They were shocked to see that fifty years after the Civil War, in many parts of the country the dark-skinned people could still not use the same toilets, drink the same water, or go to the same restaurants, hotels, and schools as the lightest-skinned people. Again, they were fascinated that a people who professed to be followers of Jesus could be so blockheaded and downright obtuse. They were no longer shocked by such nonsense as they had seen it in so many places. And when these Americans – as they called themselves – started claiming they were "God's country" and "the greatest nation on Earth", God and Naomi could only chuckle, especially since many of the people had never been to another land. But otherwise, they tended to be rather happy and jolly people, happy to have found their promised land. They watched cars and airplanes get invented, factories sprouting up everywhere, roads and airports built, hospitals and schools blossoming wherever people congregated in mass. At one point, the entire country turned into a great machine for making military equipment and preparing hundreds of thousands of new young men for battle. For the second time the European continent had turned into a human slaughterhouse. God and Naomi were relieved to be "here" and not there. They had seen enough killing.

While all this was going on, they decided to walk through every state from sea to shining sea. For the next thirty years they went to the national parks, big cities, deserts, small towns, forests, monuments, mountains, valleys, and fields. They saw Bryce Canyon in summer, the Grand Canyon at sunrise, Montana, North Dakota, Mississippi, Louis Armstrong singing *What a Wonderful World* in New Orleans, Tennessee, Nebraska, the Boston Garden, the streets of San Francisco, the Empire State building, the ghettoes of Harlem, Detroit, and Oakland, and they were even on hand when the first Disneyland opened in the middle of the orange groves of Anaheim in the mid-1950s. They didn't miss the last Beatles concert in Candlestick Park, nor did they ignore Death Valley, Yuma, Yankee Stadium, Caesar's Palace, Moonlight Ranch, Salt Lake City, the Tabernacle Choir, the Playboy Mansion, Chinatown, Denny's in Denver, the Boeing factory, the Seahawks, Chicago, Nashville, Memphis, Elvis, Fred Astaire dancing across a ceiling, the Black Panthers, John Kennedy shot in Dallas, Dr. King murdered, Bobby Kennedy's dead body on a kitchen floor in Los Angeles, Sandy Koufax pitching in Dodger Stadium, or the Rose Bowl parade in Pasadena, the beauty of Bill Russell and Wilt Chamberlain loping down the court, the Great Lakes, Niagara Falls, and New York Knicks winning the NBA crown.

Finally, after more than a hundred years of meandering through forty-eight states (they never made it to Alaska or Hawaii), on July 4th, 1973 they arrived at the nation's capital in Washington, D.C.

Actually they cheated a little and had taken a train down from New York. Two-thousand-year-olds deserve a break. When people asked them how old they really were, God would say, "I'm one thousand nine hundred and seventy-three, but she's four years younger." But the truth is, God was never entirely sure how old they were. Of course at this point it didn't really matter. He had never understood exactly how the Western world was keeping track of time with its B.C. and A.D. stuff. It seemed they used B.C. on one side of his father and A.D. on the other side. As far as he knew, B.C. meant *Before Christ*, but A.D.... what did that mean? If it meant *After the Death of Jesus*, then he was indeed exactly 1,973 years old. But other people told him that

A.D. actually meant *Anno Domini* which he knew (from his days of speaking Latin) meant something like *in the year of our Lord*. That might affect his age. He knew that in the great scheme of things none of this really mattered an iota, nor did it tell us anything whatsoever about the actual age of the earth or the universe.

Be that as it may, God and Naomi had every right to be tired after some twenty centuries on earth and the hundreds of thousands of kilometres that had passed under their feet. They reckoned they deserved that train ride down the east coast from New York.

They got to Union Station at nine-thirty in the evening, just as darkness was falling. It was the train's last stop and all the passengers disembarked. God and Naomi were struck by the relative silence in the cavernous station. Nobody was waiting on the platform to greet anybody and none of the arriving passengers expressed any joy upon meeting their destination. The herd scuttled away, the sound of footsteps echoing as people lethargically made their way toward the exits.

When Naomi and God got outside, the summer

air had a slightly metallic smell and felt like it stuck on their skin. As always, they had no idea where they were nor where they were going. They hadn't used a map for two millennia and they weren't about to start then. They began to wander down a large street. Both now limped and their gait was slow. They got to an intersection (Massachusetts Avenue and 2nd St. NE, but they didn't know it) and stopped to rest. Two young men approached them hurriedly. God noticed that one man had a knife in his hand, so he smiled and started the conversation:

Good evening gentlemen. Are you going to a dinner party? Do you have a steak or turkey to carve?

Yo, muthafuggas. We ain gah no time fo no bullshittin… Empty yo fuggin poggets.

I beg your pardon, sir. God and Naomi were normally quite good with languages. They spoke over a hundred of them and knew English quite well. But here was a new version for some fast learning.

Ah sezz gimme yo gawd dam fuggin cash rih now o weez gunna cut you mutha fuggers up. The taller man put the knife closer to God's body wanting to make sure that the old man saw the lustrous blade.

Did I hear you correctly? Did you say the word "God"? How did you know my name? It's a pleasure to meet you. What's your name?

Yo, Slim, we don give a gawddamm fugg who yo azzes be, we jus wants yo money. Under the streetlight sweat balls glistened on his ebony brow.

There you go again using my name. Thank you for your politeness. Are we to understand that you are having financial problems? We have observed that many people have financial problems here in your country. Many people in many other parts of the world share your fate…

Yo professa… we ain gah no time ta be talkin' bout no fuggin state uh da gawd damm wuld…

I am like my father… Jesus. You might have heard of him yourself … He gave everything he had to the poor. He would give his shoes or the shirt off his back if another man needed it.

Ah don giv a fugg who yo daddy be and wez don need no fuggin clothes… and wez gah plenia shooz…

I see, sir, but I must tell you that Naomi and I have not had money for almost two thousand years.

Wha da fugg!… Ain had no money fo how long? You shu be da wuns shuh be fuggin robbin us! The two men looked at each other laughed.

My dear friends… What are your names?

Yo… Gawd… dat yo name, ain it?... Yuz gotz ta be wunna da funniest sunzzabitches ize evah seen. Ha ole you say yo azz iz?

Approximately one thousand nine hundred and seventy-three years old. It might depend on who's counting.

Gaw damm… I canst even coun da fuggin far…

I must correct you. My last name is not Damn. I normally don't use a last name. But if you insist, Christ would be mine.

Yo name be Gaw Christ! Holy fugg!!! Yo… listen man… Ah gots a serius queshun fo ya…Whe yo azz live? He motioned to his friend to put the knife away.

We just live on the earth. We have no home. We have been walking all over the world for almost two thousand years. We originally left Palestine when my mother died and when Naomi's father beat her severely because she wouldn't marry the man he had chosen for her.

Nah ain dat sum shiiit… leas she had a fuggin father. Ah ain neva see mine.

Listen, my friends, Naomi and I are very hungry

and thirsty? Are you hungry? Maybe we could look for some food together. And why don't we go somewhere where we can sit down and talk? And at least have a glass of water

Yo Mustang… (he addressed his partner in life and crime)*… Iz thinkin' ma mudda wu luv ta mee dis muthafugga an his ole lady…*

Yo Tiga… Ah think yooz ri…

And so it came to pass that Anthony "Tiger" Taylor and Michael "Mustang" Jones took God and Mary on the cross-town bus to the southeast part of the city where Anthony's mother greeted them in her semi-rundown ghetto home. She gave them food and a place to sleep. She was as kind and hospitable as anybody they had met on their voyage. While they were eating biscuits and sipping hot chocolate, she told God and Naomi about how she prayed to the Good Lord every night to keep her children out of jail… *"Ders anuf ghetto kiz in der…Dey don needs no mo. Ma boy Tony awready bin in der twice… an daz two time too many!"* Anthony was the oldest of her five children.

By the time they finished their snack, it was after midnight and it was apparent that Naomi and God were very tired. Mrs. Taylor took them to her bedroom. She gave them her bed and wouldn't hear of any other solution for the night's sleeping arrangements. She would be fine on the couch.

LXXXVI

Since her husband disappeared, Loretta Taylor works two jobs six days a week. She leaves at five in the morning for her job at the high school where she sweeps floors and washes windows until noon; then at one she hops on a bus to the Hamilton Hotel where she changes sheets, vacuums carpets, keeps things shiny. Before going to sleep that night with her guests, God and Naomi, she says, *So you fokes jus may yoseves ri at home. Ders plenny fo brefus in da frige an ders cereal in da cubud.*

Thank you. It's so kind of you to take us in like this. We won't stay long.

Ih ain evy day, I gets ta have a man named God in ma houz. Iz you relly two thousan yiz ol?

It's been a long road.

You dun musta seen a ho la in yo day.

We've seen a few things.

Okay… Iz gotsta ta ge up erly fo wuk. If dem kizz mess up tumaha, you spank der bottoms pink.

I'm sure they'll be fine. We might be gone before you get back…

You duze whah you wan. Bu yooz wecome to stay az long az you likes. Iz gotsta ge some sleep. Wuz nice meetin yall.

They hear her go out the door at five, but sleep for another two hours. When they get up and tiptoe downstairs to the kitchen, the rest of the house is silent. As they sip their coffee the youngest, little Latisha, staggers into the room with her teddy bear. She does not seem to be surprised to see the two strangers. She says *good morning* and turns on the TV. Cartoons fill the screen. A few minutes later Dontaye shows up and without a word installs himself next to his sister on the couch. He has a rag in his hand and puts a thumb in the mouth. He must be about eight. Naomi stands and offers the children juice and donuts that she has found in the refrigerator. Both decline with a wag of the head. A few minutes later, a hurricane floats down the stairs.

As soon as he sets eyes on the strangers the whole atmosphere changes…

Who ah you? Wher you cum from? Yuz luh li misser and missus Muthuzala who be livin bout nih hured yir. He talks like a machine gun.

We came in last night with your brother Anthony. We met him on the street.

Ah beh he tri ta rob yo azz.

That might have been his original intention, but he ended up being a most pleasant fellow.

Wher you dun learn ta talk lak da?

It's not important. What might your name be?

Jerry. Da one an ony Jerry. All fo fee fo inches uh me. So I seez yuz met Tish and Dontaye.

Not really. But they're adorable children.

They ain ta much cuz thez kinna shy.

Jerry helps himself to a bowl of Wheaties. He sits down at the table with God and Naomi.

So howz you ge so old? Ah ha a grampa who gotz ta be bout niney-fi, bu you gah him be by a mile. Wher you cum from eyway?

We were in New York yesterday. We've been walking around the world for a long time.

Da wuld! Shi, I ain been outta D.C.

From what we hear, you have a lot of nice

monuments here in the nation's capital.

Ya, bu I ain neva seen nun of em.

You haven't seen any of the monuments in Washington, D.C.?

Nope. Who gunna tay me? Sanna Claus? Ain nobuey gunna sho me no monaments here. Momma wuk ah day. I seen em on TV doh.

Jerry pours more milk on his cereal.

Now Jerry, how old are you?

Ten.

So you're in school...

Na now. Dis ih summa vacashun... but den we gah sku again.

What grade are you in?

Ah be starrin fi grade.

Fifth grade?

Yeah.

That's wonderful. Do you like school?

Ain do nuttin bu mez aroun...

God decides he will do a little social anthropology. They are in the nation's capital, probably only a few hundred metres from the Capitol Building itself. He will ask Jerry a few questions to see what he has learned so far in school. The boy obviously has a very quick mind.

Jerry, let me ask you a question or two. First, that milk you just poured on your cereal... where does it come from?

Fru da sto.

I know it comes from the store. But before it comes to the store, where is it made?

In a mil fatory.

It is made in a milk factory?

Wher da hell elz ih gunna be made?

Jerry, milk comes from cows.

Shiiiiiiii... mil don come fru no cow...

It really does. Maybe we can take you to a farm where you can see real cows.

Nobuey neva ta me nowher... I ain neva been ouside da neybahood.

You've never been outside of your neighbourhood?

Nope.

God looks around the room for a pencil and a piece of paper. He finds both next to the telephone. *Okay Jerry. Here's a piece of paper and a pencil. Now I'm going to dictate a few sentences to you. You write down what I say. Okay, are you ready?*

Jerry doesn't say anything. He puts his spoon down, picks up the pencil and stares at the white piece of paper.

My…name…is…Jerry…I…live…in…Wash-ington D. C.

Jerry's hand doesn't move.

Jerry, write what I say. This is just for fun. I'm not going to give you a grade or anything. MY…NAME…IS…JERRY…I…LIVE…IN…WASH…

Jerry looks at God.

Yo… Gawd. … I ca ri nuttin. I ain neva learn howda ri.

You mean you're going into the fifth grade and you haven't learned to write?

No suh…

There is a hint of shame on Jerry's face.

Can you read?

I ca read needa.

You haven't learned how to read either?

Nah rilly.

Jerry, what do you do in school all day? Don't you have books and exercises and things?

Wez ony ga a cuppla boo fo all da class… we don do nuttin in sku…

Naomi looks at Jerry, then at his brother and sister curled up on the couch watching cartoons. These are real children with real lives. Anthony, the practicing delinquent, is still asleep upstairs. There is an older sister, too. None of these kids have asked to be born. None asked to be born where they were born. What will happen to them? What kind of lives will they have? She looks at God. They are both filled with love. What else can one be filled with when one sees such conditions? The whole world is innocent. They both know it. They have seen more of the world than any two people who have ever lived. Every single solitary drop of existence is as innocent as rain. The world turns and turns. How long has it been turning? Nobody knows. Nobody will ever know. Nothing in existence can know existence. But it isn't just the world that is turning. Everything is turning. Time, space, bodies, minds, atoms, planets, galaxies, clocks, generations, life, death. It is all innocent. Nothing asks to be what it is. All is virginal. This is the great lesson she and God have learned after two thousand years of existence. Things are what they are. Everything. The best to the worst. The happiest to the saddest. The most fortunate to the least fortunate. Nothing can stop the world. It will go where it will go. If people want to believe there is a grand god in the sky who loves and protects them, let them. In any case, they will believe what they believe. If Latisha and Dontaye want to sit on the couch all day and watch cartoons, let them… Naomi is overcome by a great sadness, but also a great liberation. God looks at her. They both know what she is feeling. What can one do? She knows there is a better life than watching TV all day. She knows there is a better life than robbing innocent people in the street. She knows there is a better life than not being able to read or write at age ten. But what can she do? Can she educate these children? Should she and God spend the rest of their lives right there in Loretta Taylor's house trying to help these kids? She and God know they are going to die soon. Two thousand years has been enough. They have seen more and loved each other more than any two people in the history of the world. Can they really help these kids? Can they help Loretta Taylor? They could cook and clean while she works. They could educate the kids. But what does it mean to "educate" someone? Probably less than one kilometre from where they are is the building that houses the Congress of the United States of America, the most powerful nation in the world. It is filled with so-called "educated" men and women.

But are they really "educated"? Are their lives better than any other lives? Are they happier? Don't they believe in all kinds of lies like justice, free will, God, history? Aren't most of the members of congress frustrated in their marriages? Don't they all want more? More money? More power? More votes? Bigger cars? Bigger houses? Another lover? Reelection? Headlines? … Naomi thinks about the world. God is thinking with her. They sit at that table with Jerry. They put out their hands and touch each other's fingers. The touch of love. They love each other. They love Jerry, Dontaye, and Latisha. They love the world. They love existence. All of it. The whole glorious salmagundi. The whole heaven. The whole hell. The whole beauty. The whole monstrousness. In the end, isn't existence kind of an all or nothing deal? If it's all tied together, if there is no beginning and no end, if there is no real "history", if every moment is infinite, if nothing can be other than what it is, if the whole bag of marbles really is just there… forever and ever… then if one piece was gone, the whole thing would be gone.

As Naomi and God hold hands and look around the room, they think about all they have seen in those two thousand years. All the suffering, all the killing, one group controlling another, the armies, the inquisitions, the conquests, the slaves, the kings, the concubines, the Jews, the Romans, the Greeks, the Vietnamese, the Chinese, the Mongolians, the Turks, the Africans, the Spanish, the Portuguese, the Indians, the French, the English, the Aztecs, Incas, Mayans, and the Americans. It is all one very slow-moving process. Life on this earth is one huge labourious snail that oozes through time and space, slowly, ever so slowly, moving from point A to point B. Here they are in the capital of great America and there are children in 1973 who can't read or write, children who have never been more than two miles from their home, children whose mother works twelve hours a day and whose older brother is a delinquent. The slaves that were taken from Africa are still here; their form had just changed. And even aren't the men and women across the park in the Capitol Building a different kind of slave? Aren't they slaves to their own pasts just like Jerry, Latisha, and Dontaye are slaves to theirs? They are slaves to their religions, their places, their positions, their values, their principles.

The snail is eking its way across deserts and

jungles, forests, mountains, valleys, oceans, cities. The living and the dead are everywhere.

God and Naomi join the latter group not long after their stay with Loretta Taylor and her family. They leave Washington, D. C. that morning around eleven and take a greyhound bus westward bound. They are too tired to walk any more. After three days of travel they are at the Grand Canyon. They want to see it one more time. From there they write a letter to Jerry Taylor:

Dear Jerry (and Loretta and family),
Thanks for letting us stay with you. We enjoyed every second of our visit. Jerry, we know you can't read this letter, but we want you to have your mother (or somebody else if she can't read) read it to you over and over and over until you can understand it and read it back to her. It could be a start to you having a better life. What is a better life? What is a good life? Though we have seen more of the world than any two people ever to live, we cannot answer these questions for you. Each person must respond for himself or herself. There are as many different answers as there are people on Earth.

You come from the D.C ghetto. Your brother Anthony is already a criminal. He'll probably end up in prison or dead on a sidewalk. This is sad because he seems like he could be a very nice fellow. Maybe this letter might even help him… and his friend Mustang. We don't know. One never knows whom or what one really helps. All you can do is try.

What we want to tell you, Jerry, is that it is very possible that you only have one life to live and then you die and are gone forever. People talk a lot about gods, Jesus, a resurrection, an afterlife, etc. We are sure you have seen those evangelist Christian pastors on television on Sunday morning. But Jerry, it is very probable that everything they say is a lie. No one knows for sure what happens when a person or an animal or anything dies.

Our hope is that you make the best of your time on Earth, whatever that means. Don't just follow the crowd. Be Jerry. Be unique. We also suggest that, if possible, you try not to make life miserable or unpleasant for those around you. There is enough suffering and pain as it is. Just look at your mom and how hard she works. Would you want to make things any harder for her?

You're what? Ten years old Jerry? If you're lucky, you'll have another seventy years to do things. You're a very intelligent boy. You have a good strong body and a wonderful mind. Use that mind and your body. And, if possible, use them to love.

What is love? You'll have to find that out for yourself.

Jerry, from what we know life is a great mystery. You are part of that mystery. Those cows that make the milk you put on your Wheaties are also part of that mystery. Open your eyes. Try to smile at the world. It is all we have.

Thanks again and may Jerry bless Jerry,

Your friends, Naomi & God

After posting the letter at the lodge, they walk to the rim of the canyon. God climbs first over the little guardrail, then helps Naomi. Neither look down. They embrace. And then, hand in hand and their eyes locked, they step out.

The onlookers *ooh* and *aah* and many scream with horror. Of course, they have no idea what they are seeing.

BOOKS BY JON FERGUSON

(Published by Huge Jam, 2022)

Adam's Cane
Foster's Depression
The Last Day Forever
Jesus & Mary
Mary & God
God & Naomi
The Flood
The Anthropologist

Out soon by the same author:

The Old Man and the Stone
Don't Bullshit Me Daddy

www.hugejam.com
www.jonfergusonbooks.com

ABOUT THE AUTHOR

Jon Ferguson was born in October 1949 in Oakland, California, into a devout Christian family, much like his favourite philosopher, Friedrich Nietzsche. In fact, as a child, church services were held in the family living room. At age 17, his passion for sport was almost usurped by a keenness to save the world when he enrolled at the Mormon-owned Brigham Young University. Little by little, though, he realized that if Jesus couldn't do it, neither could he. His faith in divinity began to crumble. With an adieu to the US academic world where he'd been immersed in anthropology and philosophy – and with a desire to engage with the world at large – Ferguson hopped on a plane in 1973 and by chance ended up in Nyon, Switzerland where he was soon playing basketball in the top Swiss league, becoming a key player in what fans consider to have been the golden age.

Half a century later, still in Switzerland, he is now just as well known for his writing (eighteen books published in French) as for his coaching (thirty years' worth). He's won more games than any coach in Swiss basketball history, but he likes to remind people that he lost more than everyone else as well... He has written over twenty novels and a book on Nietzsche, *Nietzsche au Petit Déjeuner (Nietzsche for Breakfast)* and a book on the history of Swiss basketball, *Of Hoops and Men.* For twenty-five years he also wrote a bi-weekly column in the Lausanne newspaper called "Ainsi Parla Schmaltz". His novel *Farley's Jewel* (Cinco Puntos Press, 1998) won a Barnes & Noble "Discover Great New Writers of America" prize.